John S. Farmer

Musa Pedestris

Three centuries of canting songs and slang rhymes - 1536-1896

John S. Farmer

Musa Pedestris
Three centuries of canting songs and slang rhymes - 1536-1896

ISBN/EAN: 9783337264468

Printed in Europe, USA, Canada, Australia, Japan

Cover: Foto ©Andreas Hilbeck / pixelio.de

More available books at **www.hansebooks.com**

Musa Pedestris.

THREE CENTURIES OF

CANTING SONGS AND SLANG RHYMES

[1536—1896]

COLLECTED AND ANNOTATED

BY

JOHN S. FARMER

PRIVATELY PRINTED FOR SUBSCRIBERS ONLY
MDCCCXCVI

CONTENTS

CONTENTS

CONTENTS

CONTENTS

INDEX TO AUTHORS

FOREWORDS

FOREWORDS

WHEN Harrison Ainsworth, in his preface to
Rookwood, claimed to be "the first to write a
purely flash song" he was very wide of the mark.
As a matter of fact, "Nix my doll, pals, fake
away!" had been anticipated, in its treatment of
canting phraseology, by nearly three centuries,
and subsequently, by authors whose names stand
high, in other respects, in English literature.

The mistake, however, was not altogether un-
pardonable; few, indeed, would have even guessed
that the appearance of utter neglect which sur-
rounded the use of Cant and Slang in English
song, ballad, or verse—its rich and racy character
notwithstanding—was anything but of the surface.
The *chanson d'argot* of France and the *romance
di germania* of Spain, not to mention other forms
of the MUSA PEDESTRIS had long held popular
sway, but there was to all appearance nothing
to correspond with them on this side the silver
streak.

It must be confessed, however, that the field
of English slang verse and canting song, though

not altogether barren, has yet small claim to the idiomatic and plastic treatment that obtains in many an *Argot-song* and *Germania-romance*; in truth, with a few notable exceptions, there is little in the present collection that can claim literary rank.

Those exceptions, however, are alone held to be ample justification for such an anthology as that here presented. Moreover these "Rhymes and Songs", gathered from up and down the years, exhibit, *en masse*, points of interest to the student and scholar that, in isolation, were either wanting altogether, or were buried and lost sight of midst a mass of more (or less) valuable matter.

As regards the Vulgar Tongue itself—though exhaustive disquisition obviously lies outside the scope of necessarily brief forewords—it may be pointed out that its origin in England is confessedly obscure. Prior to the second half of the 16th century, there was little trace of that flood of unorthodox speech which, in this year of grace eighteen hundred and ninety-six, requires six quarto double-columned volumes duly to chronicle—verily a vast and motley crowd!

As to the distinction to be drawn between Cant and Slang it is somewhat difficult to speak. Cant we know; its limits and place in the world of philology are well defined. In Slang, however, we have a veritable Proteus, ever shifting, and for the most part defying exact definition and orderly derivation. Few, save scholars and such-like

folk, even distinguish between the two, though
the line of demarcation is sharply enough defined.

In the first place, Slang is universal, whilst
Cant is restricted in usage to certain classes of
the community: thieves, vagrom men, and—well,
their associates. One thing, indeed, both have
in common; each are derived from a correct
normal use of language. There, however, all
similarity ends.

Slang boasts a quasi-respectability denied to
Cant, though Cant is frequently more enduring,
its use continuing without variation of meaning
for many generations. With Slang this is the
exception; present in force to-day, it is either
altogether forgotten to-morrow, or has shaded off
into some new meaning—a creation of chance
and circumstance. Both Cant and Slang, but
Slang to a more determinate degree, are mirrors
in which those who look may see reflected a
picture of the age, with its failings, foibles, and
idiosyncrasies. They reflect the social life of the
people, the mirror rarely being held to truth so
faithfully—hence the present interest, and may
be future value, of these songs andrhymes. For
the rest the book will speak for itself.

Musa Pedestris.

RHYMES OF THE CANTING CREW.

[Notes]

[*c.* 1536]

[From "*The Hye-way to the Spyttel-hous*" by
ROBERT COPLAND (HAZLITT, *Early Popular
Poetry of England, iv.*) ROBERT COPLAND
and the Porter of St. Bartholomew's Hospital *loquitor*].

Copland. Come none of these pedlers this way
                             [also,
With pak on bak with their bousy spéche   *crapulous*
Jagged and ragged with broken hose and breche?

Porter. Inow, ynow; with bousy coue maimed nace,   [Notes]
Teare the patryng coue in the darkeman cace
Docked the dell for a coper meke;

I

His watch shall feng a prounces nob-chete,
Cyarum, by Salmon, and thou shall pek my jere
In thy gan, for my watch it is nace gere
For the bene bouse my watch hath a coyn.

And thus they babble tyll their thryft is thin
I wote not what with their pedlyng frenche.

THE BEGGAR'S CURSE   [Notes]

[1608]

[From *Lanthorne and Candlelight*, by THOMAS
DEKKER, ed. GROSART (188), iii, 203:—"a
canting song, wherein you may learn, how
this cursed *generation* pray, or (to speake
truth) curse such officers as punish them"].

I

The Ruffin cly the nab of the Harmanbeck,

If we mawnd Pannam, lap, or Ruff-peck,

Or poplars of yarum : he cuts, bing to the Ruffmans,

Or els he sweares by the light-mans,

To put our stamps in the Harmans,

The ruffian cly the ghost of the Harmanbeck

If we heaue a booth we cly the Ierk.

Side notes:
The devil take the Constable's head!
If we beg bread, drink, bacon.
Or milk porridge, he says: "be off to the hedges"
Or swears, in the morning
To clap our feet in the stocks.
The devil take the Constable's ghost
If we rob a house we are flogged.

II

If we niggle, or mill a bowzing Ken,

Or nip a boung that has but a win,

Side notes:
If we fornicate, or thieve in an ale-house.
Rob a purse with only a penny in it.

Or break into a gentleman's house,

Or dup the giger of a Gentry cofes ken,

To the magistrate we go;

To the quier cuffing we bing;

Then to gaol to be shackled,

And then to the quier Ken, to scowre the Cramp-ring,

Whence to be hanged on the gallows in the morning.

And then to the 'Trin'de on the chates, in the light-

[mans.

The pox and the devil take the Constable and his stocks.

The Bube & Ruffian cly the Harmanbeck

& harmans.

"TOWRE OUT BEN MORTS" [Notes]

[1610]

[By SAMUEL ROWLANDS in "*Martin Mark-all,
Beadle of Bridewell: His Defence and Answere
to the Belman of London*"].

I

Towre out ben morts & towre,   look-out, good women;

Looke out ben morts & towre,   all the Rome-coves [Notes]

For all the Rome coues are budgd a beake,   have run away [Notes]

And the quire coves tippe the lowre.   Queer-coves taken the money.

II

The quire coues are budgd to the bowsing ken,   have sneaked to the ale-house,

As Romely as a ball,   nimbly

But if we be spid we shall be clyd,   whipped

And carried to the quirken hall.   taken to gaol.

III

crept; master of the house;
Out budgd the Coue of the ken,

staff; hand.
With a ben filtch in his quarr'me

went to search for the man who had given the alarm.
That did the prigg good that bingd in the kisome,

To towre the Coue budge alar'me.

THE MAUNDER'S WOOING   [Notes]
[1610]

[By Samuel Rowlands in *Martin Mark-all,
Beadle of Bridewell: His Defence and Answere
to the Belman of London:*—"I will shew you
what I heard at *Knock-vergos*, drinking there
a pot of English Ale, two Maunders borne and
bred vp rogues wooing in their natiue language "].

I

O Ben mort wilt thou pad with me,   good   woman tramp
One ben slate shall serue both thee and me,   sheet
My Caster and Commission shall serue vs both to   cloak; shirt; beg
[maund,
My bong, my lowre & fambling cheates   purse; money; rings
Shall be at thy command.

II

O Ben Coue that may not be,   good man
For thou hast an Autem mort who euer that is she,   wife
If that she were dead & bingd to his long tibb,   gone to her long-home
Then would I pad and maund with thee,   tramp and beg
And wap and fon the fibb.   [Notes]

III

find out   O ben mort Castle out & Towre,

thieves; conge-   Where all the Roome coues slopne that we may
grate; get money: [tip the lowre,

sold the swag   Whē we haue tipt the lowre & fenc't away the duds

go to the ale-   Then binge we to the bowzing ken,
house

called the "Robin   Thats cut the Robin Hood.
Hood."

IV

arrested?   But O ben Coue what if we be clyd,

cheat and steal   Long we cannot foist & nip at last we shall be
                             [spyed,

If that we be spied, O then begins our woe,

magistrate   With the Harman beake out and alas,

Newgate   To VVittington we goe.

V

Hold your jaw!   Stow your whids & plant, and whid no more
bide, and say no
more   [of that

[Notes]   Budg a beak the cracknās & tip lowr with thy prat

hanging; pick a   If treyning thou dost feare, thou ner wilt foist
purse   [a Ian,

rob; whore; hang   Then mill, and wap and treine for me,

[Notes]   A gere peck in thy gan.

[Notes]   As they were thus after a strange maner a
wooing, in comes by chance a clapper-dudgeon
for a pinte of Ale, who as soone as he was spied,

they left off their roguish poetry, and fell to mocke
the poor maunder thus.

VI

The clapper dugeon lies in the skipper,   beggar; barn
He dares not come out for shame,
But when he binges out he dus budg to the gigger,   comes out; goes to people's doors—
Tip in my skew good dame.   "Put something in my wallet."

[Notes]   "A GAGE OF BEN ROM-BOUSE"
[1611]

[By MIDDLETON and DEKKER in "*The Roaring Girl*"
v. 1. Sung by *Moll-Cut-purse* and *Tearcat*
a bullying rogue.]

Moll. Come you rogue, sing with me: —

A pot of strong ale (or wine)   A gage of ben Rom-bouse,

London ale-house   In a bousing-ken of Rom-vile

better than a cloak   *Tearcat.* Is benar than a Caster,

meat,bread,drink, or porridge   Peck, pennam, lap, or popler,

steal on the country-side.   Which we mill in deuse a vile.

lie all day   *Moll.* Oh, I wud lib all the lightmans,

night   Oh, I woud lib all the darkemans,

By the mass! in the woods   By the salomon, under the Ruffemans

stocks   By the salomon in the Hartmans

in fetters   *Tearcat.* And scoure the queer cramp ring

[Notes]   And couch till a palliard dock'd my dell,

addle-pate may swill strong drink   So my bousy nab might skew rome bouse well

Let us be off on the road.   { Avast to the pad, let us bing;
{ Avast to the pad, let us bing.

"BING OUT, BIEN MORTS" [Notes]

[1612]

[From *O per se O*, by THOMAS DEKKER].

Bing out, bien Morts, and toure, and toure,

    bing out, bien Morts, and toure;

For all your Duds are bingd awaste,

    the bien coue hath the loure.

Go abroad, good women, and look about you; For all your clothes are stolen; and a good fellow (a clever thief) has the money.

I

I met a Dell, I viewde her well,

    she was benship to my watch;

So she and I, did stall and cloy,

    whateuer we could catch.

I met a wench and summed her up, she suited me very well So (joining company) she watched while I stole whatever came our way.

II

This Doxie dell, can cut bien whids,

    and wap well for a win;

And prig and cloy so benshiply,

    all the dewsea-vile within.

This young whore can lie like truth, fornicate vigorously for a penny And steal very cleverly on the country-side

III

The boyle was vp, wee had good lucke,

in frost, for and in snow;

When they did seeke, then we did creepe,

and plant in ruffe-mans low.

IV

To Stawling Kenne the Mort bings then,

to fetch loure for her cheates;

Duds and Ruff-pecke, rumboild by Harmanbecke,

and won by Mawnder's feates.

V

You Mawnders all, stow what you stall,

to Rome coues watch so quire;

And wapping Dell that niggles well,

and takes loure for her hire.

VI

And Jybe well Ierkt, tick rome-comfeck,

for backe by glimmar to mawnd,

To mill each Ken, let coue bing then,

through ruffemans, lague or launde.

VII

Till Cramprings quier, tip Coue his hire,

    and quier-kens doe them catch;

A canniken, mill quier cuffen,

    so quier to ben coue's watch.

Till fetters are his deserts and a prison is his fate A plague take the magistrate! who is so hard on a clever rogue

VIII

Bein darkmans then, bouse, mort, and ken

    the bien coue's bingd awast;

On chates to trine, by Rome-coues dine

    for his long lib at last.

A good-night then to drink, wench, and ale-house— the poor fellow is gone On the gallows to hang by rogues betray'd to his long sleep.

Bingd out bien morts, and toure, and toure,

    bing out of the Rome-vile;

And toure the coue, that cloyde your duds,

    upon the chates to trine.

So go, my good woman out of London And see the man who stole your clothes upon the gallows hanging.

THE SONG OF THE BEGGAR
[1620]

[From "*A Description of Love*" 6th ed. (1629)].

I

I am Rogue and a stout one,
    A most courageous drinker,
I doe excell, 'tis knowne full well,
    The Ratter, Tom, and Tinker.
        Still doe I cry, good your Worship good
penny   Bestow one small Denire, Sir [Sir,
ale-house   And brauely at the bousing Ken
drink   Ile bouse it all in Beere, Sir.

II

purse; [Notes]   If a Bung be got by the hie Law,
    Then straight I doe attend them,
For if Hue and Crie doe follow, I
    A wrong way soone doe send them.
        Still doe I cry, etc.

III

Ten miles vnto a Market.
    I runne to meet a Miser,

Then in a throng, I nip his Bung,   steal his purse
  And the partie ne'er the wiser.
    Still doe I cry, etc.

IV

My dainty Dals, my Doxis,   girls; whores
  Whene'er they see me lacking,
Without delay, poore wretches they
  Will set their Duds a packing.   pawn their clothes
    Still doe I cry, etc.

V

I pay for what I call for,
  And so perforce it must be,
For as yet I can, not know the man,
  Nor Oastis that will trust me.
    Still doe I cry, etc.

VI

If any giue me lodging,
  A courteous Knaue they find me,
For in their bed, aliue or dead,
  I leave some Lice behind me.
    Still doe I cry, etc.

VII

If a Gentry Coue be comming,   gentleman
  Then straight it is our fashion,

My Legge I tie, close to my thigh,
  To moue him to compassion.
    Still doe I cry, etc.

VIII

My doublet sleeue hangs emptie,
  And for to begge the bolder,
For meate and drinke mine arme I shrinke,
  Vp close vnto my shoulder.
    Still doe I cry, etc.

IX

If a Coach I heere be rumbling,
  To my Crutches then I hie me,
For being lame, it is a shame,
  Such Gallants should denie me.
    Still doe I cry, etc.

X

With a seeming bursten belly,
  I looke like one half dead, Sir,
Or else I beg with a woodden legge,
  And a Night-cap on me head, Sir,
    Still doe I cry, etc.

XI

In Winter time starke naked
  I come into some Citie,
Then euery man that spare them can,

Will giue me clothes for pittie.
　　Still doe I cry, etc.

XII

If from out the Low-countrie, [Notes]
　　I heare a Captaines name, Sir,
Then strait I swere I have bin there;
　　And so in fight came lame, Sir.
　　　Still doe I cry, etc.

XIII

My Dogge in a string doth lead me,
　　When in the towne I goe, Sir,
For to the blind, all men are kind,
　　And will their Almes bestow, Sir,
　　　Still doe I cry, etc.

XIV

With Switches sometimes stand I,
　　In the bottom of a Hill, Sir,
There those men which doe want a switch,
　　Some monie give me still, Sir.
　　　Still doe I cry, etc.

XV

Come buy, come buy a Horne-booke,
　　Who buys my Pins or Needles?
In Cities I these things doe crie,

2

Oft times to scape the Beadles.
Still doe I cry, etc.

XVI

[Notes]

In Pauls Church by a Pillar;
Sometimes you see me stand, Sir,
With a Writ that showes, what care and woes
I past by Sea and Land, Sir.
Still doe I cry, etc.

XVII

Now blame me not for boasting,
And bragging thus alone, Sir,
For my selfe I will be praying still,
For Neighbours have I none, Sir.
Which makes me cry, etc.

THE MAUNDER'S INITIATION
[1622]

[Notes]

[From *The Beggar's Bush* by JOHN FLETCHER ;
also in *The New Canting Dict:*—" Sung on
the electing of a new dimber damber, or
king of the gypsies"].

I

Cast your nabs and cares away,
   This is maunder's holiday: beggar
   In the world look out and see,
   Where so blest a king as he
     (*Pointing to the newly-elected Prince.*)

II

At the crowning of our king,
   Thus we ever dance and sing:
   Where's the nation lives so free,
   And so merrily as we?

III

Be it peace, or be it war,
   Here at liberty we are:
   Hang all harmanbecks we cry,   constables
   We the cuffins quere defy.   magistrates

IV

We enjoy our ease and rest,
　　To the fields we are not pressed:
　　And when taxes are increased,
　　We are not a penny 'sessed.

V

Nor will any go to law,
　　With a maunder for a straw,
　　All which happiness he brags,
　　Is only owing to his rags.

" Now swear him "—

I pour on thy
pate a pot of
good ale
And install thee,
by oath, a rogue
To beg by the
way, steal from
all,
Rob hedge of
shirt and sheet,

To lie with wench-
es on the straw,
so let all magis-
trates and con-
stables go to the
devil and be
hanged!

I crown thy nab with a gage of ben bouse,

And stall thee by the salmon into clowes,

To maund on the pad, and strike all the cheats,

To mill from the Ruffmans, Commission, and
　　　　　　　　　　　　　　　[slates,

Twang dells i' th' stiromel, and let the Quire
　　　　　　　　　　　　　　　[Cuffin

And Harman Beck strine and trine to the ruffin.

THE HIGH PAD'S BOAST

[*b.* 1625]

[Attributed to JOHN FLETCHER—a song from a
collection of black-letter broadside ballads.
Also in *New Canting Dict.* 1725.]

I

I keep my Horse; I keep my whore;
I take no rents; yet am not poor;
I travel all the land about,
And yet was born to ne'er a foot.

II

With partridge plump, and woodcock fine,
At midnight, I do often dine:
And if my whore be not in Case,   in the house
My hostess' daughter has her place.

III

The maids sit up, and watch their turns;
If I stay long, the tapster mourns;
Nor has the cookmaid mind to sin,
Tho' tempted by the chamberlain.

IV

But when I knock, O how they bustle;
The hostler yawns, the geldings justle:
If the maid be sleepy, O how they curse her;
And all this comes, of, *Deliver your purse, sir.*

THE MERRY BEGGARS [Notes]
[1641]

[From *A Jovial Crew*, by RICHARD BROME. The beggars discovered at their feast. After they have scrambled awhile at their Victuals: this song].

I

Here safe in our Skipper let's cly off our Peck, Safe in our barn let's eat
And bowse in defiance o' the Harman Beck. And drink without fear of the constable!
Here's Pannam and Lap, and good Poplars of [Yarrum, Here's bread, drink, and milk-porridge
To fill up the Crib, and to comfort the Quarron. To fill the belly, and comfort the body.
Now bowse a round health to the Go-well and [Com-well, Drink a good health [Notes]
Of Cisley Bumtrincket that lies in the Strummel; To Cisley Bumtrincket lying in the straw

II

Here's Ruffpeck and Casson, and all of the best, Here's bacon and cheese,
And Scrape of the Dainties of Gentry Cofe's [Feast. And scraps from the gentleman's table

Here's pork, mutton, goose, And chicken, all well-cooked. For this good food and meat let us Drink the gentleman's health and Then drink a bumper

Here's Grunter and Bleater, with Tib-of-the-Buttry,

And Margery Prater, all dress'd without sluttry.

For all this bene Cribbing and Peck let us then,

Bowse a health to the Gentry Cofe of the Ken.

Now bowse a round health to the Go-well

and Com-well

to Cisley Bumtrincket.

Of Cisley Bumtrincket that lies in the Strum-

[mel.

A MORT'S DRINKING SONG
[1641]

[Notes]

[From *A Jovial Crew*, by RICHARD BROME: Enter
Patrico with his old wife with a wooden
bowle of drink. She is drunk. She sings:—]

I

This is bien bowse, this is bien bowse,   strong ale
   Too little is my skew.   cup or platter
I bowse no lage, but a whole gage   water; pot
   Of this I'll bowse to you.

II

This bowse is better than rom-bowse,   wine
   It sets the gan a-gigling,   mouth
The autum-mort finds better sport   wife
   In bowsing than in nigling.   fornicating
     This is bien bowse, etc.

[*She tosses off her bowle, falls back and is
carried out.*]

[Notes]

"A BEGGAR I'LL BE"

[1660—1663]

[A black-letter broadside ballad]

I

A Beggar, a Beggar, a Beggar I'll be,
There's none leads a life more jocund than he;
A Beggar I was, and a Beggar I am,
A Beggar I'll be, from a Beggar I came;
If, as it begins, our trading do fall,
We, in the Conclusion, shall Beggars be all.
Tradesmen are unfortunate in their Affairs,
And few Men are thriving but Courtiers and Play'rs.

II

[Notes]

A Craver my Father, a Maunder my Mother,
A Filer my Sister, a Filcher my Brother,
A Canter my Uncle, that car'd not for Pelf,
A Lifter my Aunt, and a Beggar myself;
In white wheaten Straw, when their Bellies were
[full,
Then was I got between a Tinker and a Trull.
And therefore a Beggar, a Beggar I'll be,
For there's none lives a Life more jocund than he

III

For such pretty Pledges, as Lullies from Hedges.   wet linen
We are not in fear to be drawn upon Sledges,
But sometimes the Whip doth make us to skip
And then we from Tything to Tything do trip;
But when in a poor Boozing-Can we do bib it,   ale-house
We stand more in dread of the Stocks than the
And therefore a merry mad Beggar I'll be [Gibbet
For when it is night in the Barn tumbles he.

IV

We throw down no Altar, nor never do falter,
So much as to change a Gold-chain for a Halter;
Though some Men do flout us, and others do doubt
We commonly bear forty Pieces about us; [us,
But many good Fellows are fine and look fiercer,
And owe for their Cloaths to the Taylor and Mercer:
And if from the Harmans I keep out my Feet,   stocks
I fear not the Compter, King's Bench, nor the Fleet.   [Notes]

V

Sometimes I do frame myself to be lame,
And when a Coach comes, I hop to my game;
We seldom miscarry, or never do marry,
By the Gown, Common-Prayer, or Cloak-Directory;
But Simon and Susan, like Birds of a Feather
They kiss, and they laugh, and so jumble together;   [Notes]

Like Pigs in the Pea-straw, intangled they lie,
Till there they beget such a bold rogue as I.

VI

When Boys do come to us, and their Intent is
To follow our Calling, we ne'er bind 'em 'Prentice;
Soon as they come to 't, we teach them to do 't,
And give them a Staff and a Wallet to boot;
beggar's patter We teach them their Lingua, to crave and to cant,
The Devil is in them if then they can want.
And he or she, that a Beggar will be,
Without any Indentures they shall be made free.

VII

We beg for our Bread, yet sometimes it happens
We fast it with Pig, Pullet, Coney, and Capons
The Church's Affairs, we are no Men-slayers,
We have no Religion, yet live by our Prayers;
But if when we beg, Men will not draw their
                                    [Purses,
We charge, and give Fire, with a Volley of
                                    [Curses;
The Devil confound your good Worship, we cry,
And such a bold brazen- fac'd Beggar am I.

VIII

We do things in Season, and have so much Reason,
We raise no Rebellion, nor never talk Treason;

We Bill all our Mates at very low rates,
While some keep their Quarters as high as the
[fates;
With Shinkin-ap-Morgan, with Blue-cap, or Teague, [Notes]
We into no Covenant enter, nor League.
And therefore a bonny bold Beggar I'll be,
For none lives a life more merry than he.

A BUDG AND SNUDG SONG

[1676 and 1712]

[From *A Warning for Housekeepers* ... by one who was a prisoner in Newgate (1676. The second version from the *Triumph of Wit* (1712)].

I

Sneaking into house and stealing anything to hand

The budge it is a delicate trade,

And a delicate trade of fame;

Accomplished the theft

For when that we have bit the bloe,

We carry away the game:

fellow catches

But if the cully nap us,

swag [properly money]

And the lurries from us take,

take us to Newgate; [Notes]

O then $\begin{Bmatrix}\text{they rub}\\\text{he rubs}\end{Bmatrix}$ us to the whitt

halfpenny

$\begin{Bmatrix}\text{And it is hardly}\\\text{Though we are not}\end{Bmatrix}$ worth a make

II

$\begin{Bmatrix}\text{But}\\\text{And}\end{Bmatrix}$ when that we come to the whitt

fetters

Our darbies to behold,

And for to $\begin{Bmatrix}\text{take our penitency}\\\text{do our penance there}\end{Bmatrix}$'

drink

$\begin{Bmatrix}\text{And}\\\text{We}\end{Bmatrix}$ boose the water cold.

But when that we come out agen
   [And the merry hick we meet]   *countryman*
We {bite the Cully of / file off with} his cole   *steal his money*

   As {we walk / he pikes} along the street.

III

[And when that we have fil'd him   *robbed*
   Perhaps of half a job;   *half a guinea*
Then every man to the boozin ken   *ale-house*
   O there to fence his hog;   *spend a shilling*
But if the cully nap us,
   And once again we get
Into the cramping. rings],   *Handcuffs and leg-shackles*
   {But we are rubbed into / To scoure them in} the whitt.

IV

And when that we come {to / unto} the whitt,
   For garnish they do cry;   *" tooting "*
{Mary, faugh, you son of a whore / We promise our lusty comrogues}
   {Ye / They} shall have it by and bye
[Then every man with his mort in his hand,   *whore*
   Does booze off his can and part,
With a kiss we part, and westward stand,
   To the nubbing cheat in a cart].   *gallows*

V

$\begin{Bmatrix}\text{But}\\\text{And}\end{Bmatrix}$ when $\begin{Bmatrix}\text{that}\\\text{—}\end{Bmatrix}$ we come to $\begin{Bmatrix}\text{Tyburn}\\\text{the nubbing cheat}\end{Bmatrix}$

For $\begin{Bmatrix}\text{going upon}\\\text{running on}\end{Bmatrix}$ the budge,

[Notes] There stands $\begin{Bmatrix}\text{Jack Catch}\\\text{Jack Ketch}\end{Bmatrix}$, that son of a $\begin{Bmatrix}\text{whore}\\\text{bitch}\end{Bmatrix}$,

That owes us all a grudge.

hung $\begin{Bmatrix}\text{And}\\\text{For}\end{Bmatrix}$ when that he hath $\begin{Bmatrix}\text{noosed}\\\text{nubbed}\end{Bmatrix}$ us,

give no money And our friends $\begin{Bmatrix}\text{tips}\\\text{tip}\end{Bmatrix}$ him no cole,

knife $\begin{Bmatrix}\text{O then he throws us in the cart}\\\text{He takes his chive and cuts us down}\end{Bmatrix}$,

And $\begin{Bmatrix}\text{tumbles}\\\text{tips}\end{Bmatrix}$ us into $\begin{Bmatrix}\text{the}\\\text{a}\end{Bmatrix}$ hole.

[Notes] [An additional stanza is given in *Bacchus and Venus* (1737), a version which moreover contains many verbal variations].

VI

But if we have a friend stand by,
   Six and eight pence for to pay,
Then they may have our bodies back,
   And carry us quite away:
For at St Giles's or St Martin's,
   A burying place is still;
And there's an end of a darkman's budge,
   And the whoreson hath his will.

THE MAUNDER'S PRAISE OF HIS   [Notes]
STROWLING MORT

[1707]

[From *The Triumph of Wit*, by J. SHIRLEY: " the
King of the Gypsies's Song, made upon his
Beloved Doxy, or Mistress;" also in *New
Canting Dict.* (1725)].

I

Doxy, oh! thy glaziers shine	mistress; eyes
As glimmar; by the Salomon!	fire; mass
No gentry mort hath prats like thine,	lady; [Notes]
No cove e'er wap'd with such a one.	[Notes]

II

White thy fambles, red thy gan,	hand; mouth
And thy quarrons dainty is;	body
Couch a hogshead with me then,	sleep
And in the darkmans clip and kiss.	night; [Notes]

III

What though I no togeman wear,	cloak
Nor commission, mish, or slate;	shirt or sheet

3

straw

in the barn; lie

Store of strammel we'll have here,
And ith' skipper lib in state.

IV

[Notes]

the devil take
the woman
otherwise
feet

stockings; revel

Wapping thou I know does love,
Else the ruffin cly the mort;
From thy stampers then remove,
Thy drawers, and let's prig in sport.

V

daylight

hen

chickens

ale-house

When the lightman up does call,
Margery prater from her nest,
And her Cackling cheats withal,
In a boozing ken we'll feast.

VI

Money; steal

pot; steal a purse

wine; drink

eat; pig

There if lour we want; I'll mill
A gage, or nip for thee a bung;
Rum booze thou shalt booze thy fill,
And crash a grunting cheat that's young.

THE RUM-MORT'S PRAISE OF HER   [Notes]
FAITHLESS MAUNDER
[1707]

[From *The Triumph of Wit*, by J. SHIRLEY: also
in *New Canting Dict.*].

I

Now my kinching-cove is gone,   little man
    By the rum-pad maundeth none,   highway;   beg-
                                        geth
Quarrons both for stump and bone,   body
    Like my clapperdogeon.   [Notes]

II

Dimber damber fare thee well,   [Notes]
    Palliards all thou didst excel,   [Notes]
And thy jockum bore the Bell,   [Notes]
    Glimmer on it never fell.   [Notes]

III

Thou the cramprings ne'er did scowre, fetters; wear
    Harmans had on thee no power,   stocks
Harmanbecks did never toure;   constables, look
    For thee, the drawers still had loure. pockets; money

IV

clothes; general plunder
magistrate

country

gallows

Duds and cheats thou oft hast won,
  Yet the cuffin quire couldst shun;
And the deuseaville didst run,
  Else the chates had thee undone.

V

[Notes]

Crank and dommerar thou couldst play,
  Or rum-maunder in one day,
And like an Abram-cove couldst pray,
  Yet pass with gybes well jerk'd away.

VI

night

hedge

fire; duck

goose

When the darkmans have been wet,
  Thou the crackmans down didst beat
For glimmer, whilst a quaking cheat,
  Or tib-o'-th'-buttry was our meat.

VII

turkey

bacon

corn

any   potable;
porridge

Red shanks then I could not lack,
  Ruff peck still hung on my Back,
Grannam ever fill'd my sack
  With lap and poplars held I tack.

VIII

dog; wooden dish

hook; counterfeit pass,
cloak

To thy bugher and thy skew,
  Filch and gybes I bid adieu,
Though thy togeman was not new,
  In it the rogue to me was true.

THE BLACK PROCESSION   [Notes]
[1712]

[From *The Triumph of Wit*, by J. SHIRLEY:—" The
twenty craftsmen, described by the notorious
thief-taker Jonathan Wild"].

I

Good people, give ear, whilst a story I tell,
Of twenty black tradesmen who were brought up
                                        [in hell,
On purpose poor people to rob of their due;
There's none shall be nooz'd if you find but one   hung
                                        true.
The first was a coiner, that stampt in a mould;
The second a voucher to put off his gold.   passer of base coin
    Toure you well; hark you well, see   Look ! be on your guard
      Where they are rubb'd,   taken
    Up·to the nubbing cheat where they are   gallows
    nubb'd.   hung

II

The third was a padder, that fell to decay,   Tramp or footpad.
Who used for to plunder upon the highway;
The fourth was a mill-ken to crack up a door,   housebreaker

He'd venture to rob both the rich and the poor,

window thief   The fifth was a glazier who when he creeps in,

valuables   To pinch all the lurry he thinks it no sin.

Toure you well, etc.

III

pickpocket; man   The sixth is a file-cly that not one cully spares,
or silly fop
sneaking-thief   The seventh a budge to track softly upstairs;
accomplice who
jostles whilst an- The eighth is a bulk, that can bulk any hick,
other robs
countryman   If the master be nabbed, then the bulk he is
                                                        [sick,

thief who hooks   The ninth is an angler, to lift up a grate
goods from shop-
windows   If he sees but the lurry his hooks he will bait.

Toure you well, etc.

IV

The tenth is a shop-lift that carries a Bob,

When he ranges the city, the shops for to rob.

public-house thief The eleventh a bubber, much used of late;

Who goes to the ale house, and steals all their
                                                        [plate,

confidence-trick   The twelfth is a beau-trap, if a cull he does
man; good-na-
tured fool   [meet,

steals all his   He nips all his cole, and turns him into the
money
Toure you well, etc.   [street.

V

[Notes]   The thirteenth a famble, false rings for to sell,

When a mob, he has bit his cole he will tell;

The fourteenth a gamester, if he sees the cull ^{an easy dupe}
            [sweet,
He presently drops down a cog in the street;   ^{a lure}
The fifteenth a prancer, whose courage is small,   ^{horse-thief}
If they catch him horse-coursing, he's nooz'd once   ^{hung}
    Toure you well, etc.   [for all.

VI

The sixteenth a sheep-napper, whose trade is   ^{sheep-stealer}
            [so deep,
If he's caught in the corn, he's marked for a   ^{as a duffer}
            [sheep;
The seventeenth a dunaker, that stoutly makes   ^{cattle-lifte}
            [vows,
To go in the country and steal all the cows;
The eighteenth a kid-napper, who spirits young
            [men,
Tho' he tips them a pike, they oft nap him again.
    Toure you well, etc.

VII

The nineteenth's a prigger of cacklers who harms,   ^{poultry-thief}
The poor country higlers, and plunders the farms;   ^{bumpkins}
He steals all their poultry, and thinks it no sin,
When into the hen-roost, in the night, he gets in;
The twentieth's a thief-catcher, so we him call,
Who if he be nabb'd will be made pay for all.
    Toure you well, etc.

[in *Bacchus and Venus* (1737) an additional stanza is given:—

VIII

members of the There's many more craftsmen whom here I could
Canting Crew
[name,
Who use such like trades, abandon'd of shame;
To the number of more than three-score on the
[whole,
Who endanger their body, and hazard their soul;
And yet, though good workmen, are seldom made
[free,
Till they ride in a cart, and be noozed on a tree.
Toure you well, hark you well, see where they are
[rubb'd,
Up to the nubbing cheat, where they are nubb'd.

FRISKY MOLL'S SONG
[1724]

[By J. HARPER, and sung by Frisky Moll in
JOHN THURMOND'S *Harlequin Sheppard* produced at Drury Lane Theatre].

I

From priggs that snaffle the prancers strong,   *steal horses*
   To you of the *Peter* Lay,   *carriage thieves*
I pray now listen a while to my song,
   How my *Boman* he kick'd away.   *fancy man or sweetheart*

II

He broke thro' all rubbs in the whitt,   *obstacles; Newgate*
   And chiv'd his darbies in twain;   *cut: fetters*
But fileing of a rumbo ken,   *Breaking into a pawn-broker's*
   My *Boman* is snabbled again.   *imprisoned*

III

I *Frisky Moll*, with my rum coll,   *good man*
   Wou'd Grub in a bowzing ken;   *eat; ale-house*
But ere for the scran he had tipt the cole,   *refreshments; paid*
   The *Harman* he came in.   *constable*

IV

ring: watch; pistols   A ſamble, a tattle, and two popps,
            Had my *Boman* when he was ta'en;
gin-shops   But had he not bouz'd in the diddle shops,
            He'd still been in Drury-Lane.

THE CANTER'S SERENADE   [Notes]

[1725]

[from *The New Canting Dictionary* :—" Sung early
in the morning, at the barn doors where
their doxies have reposed during the night"].

I

Ye morts and ye dells   women ; girls
  Come out of your cells,
And charm all the palliards about ye;   beggars [Notes]
  Here birds of all feathers,
  Through deep roads and all weathers,
Are gathered together to toute ye.

II

With faces of wallnut,
  And bladder and smallgut,
We're come scraping and singing to rouse ye;
  Rise, shake off your straw,
  And prepare you each maw   mouth
To kiss, eat, and drink till you're bouzy.   drunk,

[Notes] "RETOURE MY DEAR DELL"

[1725]

[From *The New Canting Dictionary*].

I

night   Each darkmans I pass in an old shady grove,
day ; see   And live not the lightmans I toute not my love;
know well   I surtoute every walk, which we used to pass,
lie   And couch me down weeping, and kiss the cold
[grass:
I cry out on my mort to pity my pain,
And all our vagaries remember again.

II

mistress   Didst thou know, my dear doxy, but half of the
[smart
heart   Which has seized on my panter, since thou didst
[depart;
Didst thou hear but my sighs, my complaining
[and groans,
return   Thou'dst surely retoure, and pity my moans:
Thou'dst give me new pleasure for all my
[past pain,
eyes   And I should rejoice in thy glaziers again.

III

But alas! 'tis my fear that the false *Patri-coe*   hedge-priest
Is reaping those transports are only my due:
Retoure, my dear doxy, oh, once more retoure,
And I'll do all to please thee that lies in my
[power:
    Then be kind, my dear dell, and pity my pain,
    And let me once more toute thy glaziers again

IV

On redshanks and tibs thou shalt every day dine,   turkey geese
And if it should e'er be my hard fate to trine,   hang
I never will whiddle, I never will squeck,   speak
Nor to save my colquarron endanger thy neck.   neck
    Then once more, my doxy, be kind and
[retoure,
    And thou shalt want nothing that lies in my
[power.

THE VAIN DREAMER.

[1725]

[From *The New Canting Dictionary*].

I

evening   Yest darkmans dream'd I of my dell,
    When sleep did overtake her;
pretty   It was a dimber drowsy mort,
    She slept, I durst not wake her.

II

lips   Her gans were like to coral red,
    A thousand times I kiss'd 'em;
stolen   A thousand more I might have filch'd'
    She never could have miss'd 'em.

III

hair   Her strammel, curl'd, like threads of gold,
    Hung dangling o'er the pillow;
    Great pity 'twas that one so prim,
    Should ever wear the willow.

IV

I turned down the lilly slat,   <small>white sheet</small>
    Methought she fell a screaming,
This startled me; I straight awak'd,
    And found myself but dreaming.

"WHEN MY DIMBER DELL
I COURTED"

[1725]

[From *The New Canting Dictionary*].

I

pretty wench

When my dimber dell I courted
She had youth and beauty too,
Wanton joys my heart transported,

[Notes]

And her wap was ever new.
But conquering time doth now deceive her
Which her pleasures did uphold;
All her wapping now must leave her,
For, alas! my dell's grown old.

II

Her wanton motions which invited,
Now, alas! no longer charm,

eyes

Her glaziers too are quite benighted,
Nor can any prig-star charm.
For conquering time, alas! deceives her
Which her triumphs did uphold,
And every moving beauty leaves her
Alas! my dimber dell's grown old.

III

There was a time no cull could toute her,   man; look at
    But was sure to be undone:
Nor could th' uprightman live without her,   [Notes]
    She triumph'd over every one.
      But conquering time does now deceive her,
        Which her sporting us'd t' uphold,
      All her am'rous dambers leave her,
        For, alas! the dell's grown old.

IV

All thy comfort, dimber dell,
    Is, now, since thou hast lost thy prime,
That every cull can witness well,
    Thou hast not misus'd thy time.
      There's not a prig or palliard living,
        Who has not been thy slave inroll'd.
      Then cheer thy mind, and cease thy grieving;
        Thou'st had thy time, tho' now grown old.

THE OATH OF THE CANTING CREW

[1749]

[Notes]

[From *The Life of Bampfylde Moore Carew*, by ROBERT GOADBY].

[Notes]

I, Crank Cuffin, swear to be
True to this fraternity;
That I will in all obey
Rule and order of the lay.

reveal secrets

Never blow the gab or squeak;

betray to bailiff or magistrate

Never snitch to bum or beak;
But religiously maintain
Authority of those who reign

[Notes]

Over Stop Hole Abbey green,
Be their tawny king, or queen.
In their cause alone will fight;
Think what they think, wrong or fight;
Serve them truly, and no other,
And be faithful to my brother;
Suffer none, from far or near,
With their rights to interfere;

[Notes]

No strange Abram, ruffler crack,
Hooker of another pack,

[Notes]; beggar

Rogue or rascal, frater, maunderer,

Irish toyle, or other wanderer; [Notes]
No dimber, dambler, angler, dancer,
Prig of cackler, prig of prancer;
No swigman, swaddler, clapper-dudgeon;
Cadge-gloak, curtal, or curmudgeon;
No whip-jack, palliard, patrico;
No jarkman, be he high or low;
No dummerar, or romany;
No member of *the family*;
No ballad-basket, bouncing buffer,
Nor any other, will I suffer;
But stall-off now and for ever
All outtiers whatsoever;
And as I keep to the foregone,
So may help me Salamon! By the mass!

[Notes] COME ALL YOU BUFFERS GAY

[1760]

[From *The Humourist* . . . . a choice collection of
songs. 'A New Flash Song', p. 2].

I

rogue or horse- Come all you buffers gay,
thief
prowl about   That rumly do pad the city,
Come listen to what I do say,
    And it will make you wond'rous wity.

II

The praps are at Drury Lane,
    And at Covent Garden also,
Therefore I tell you plain,
    It will not be safe for to go.

III

well-dressed vic- But if after a rum cull you pad
tim; walk
    Pray follow him brave and bold;
For many a buffer has been grab'd,
    For fear, as I've been told.

IV

Let your pal that follows behind,
    Tip your bulk pretty soon;
And to slap his whip in time,
    For fear the cull should be down.

give signal to confederate

[Notes]

V

For if the cull should be down
    And catch you a fileing his bag,
Then at the Old Bailey you're found,
    And d—m you, he'll tip you the lag.

robbing.

get you transported

VI

But if you should slape his staunch wipe
    Then away to the fence you may go,
From thence to the ken of one T—
    Where you in full bumpers may flow.

steal; handkerchief

receiver of stolen property

house

VII

But now I have finish'd my rhime,
    And of you all must take my leave;
I would have you to leave off in time,
    Or they will make your poor hearts to bleed.

THE POTATO MAN
[1775]

[from *The Ranelaugh Concert* ...a choice collection of the newest songs sung at all the public places of entertainment].

I

I am a saucy rolling blade,
  I fear not wet nor dry,
I keep a jack ass for my trade,
  And thro' the streets do cry
    Chorus. And they all rare potatoes be!
    And they're, etc.

II

A moll I keep that sells fine fruit,
  There's no one brings more cly;
She has all things the seasons suit,
  While I my potatoes cry.
    Chorus. And they all, etc.

III

A link boy once I stood the gag,
  At Charing Cross did ply,

Marginal notes:
[Notes]
fellow
mistress
money [Notes]
cry out

Here's light your honor for a mag,   halfpenny
   But now my potatoes cry.
      Chorus. And they all, etc.

IV

With a blue bird's eye about my squeeg,   handkerchief
                                     [Notes] neck.
   And a check shirt on my back,
A pair of large wedges in my hoofs,
   And an oil skin round my hat.
      Chorus. And they all, etc.

V

I'll bait a bull or fight a cock,
   Or pigeons I will fly;
I'm up to all your knowing rigs   smart tricks
   Whilst I my potatoes cry.
      Chorus. And they all, etc.

VI

There's five pounds two-pence honest weight
   Your own scales take and try;
For nibbing culls I always hate,   cheating dealers
   And I in safety cry.
      Chorus. And they all, etc.

A SLANG PASTORAL

[1780]

[By R. Tomlinson:—a Parody on a poem by
Dr. Byrom, "My time, O ye muses, was
happily spent"].

I

companions

accompanied

My time, O ye kiddies, was happily spent,
When Nancy trigg'd with me wherever I went;
Ten thousand sweet joys ev'ry night did we prove;
Sure never poor fellow like me was in love!

jailed

But since she is nabb'd, and has left me behind,
What a marvellous change on a sudden I find!
When the constable held her as fast as could be,
I thought 'twas Bet Spriggins; but damme 'twas she.

II

With such a companion, a green-stall to keep,

drink

To swig porter all day, on a flock-bed to sleep,

ight-hearted

I was so good-natur'd, so bobbish and gay,
And I still was as smart as a carrot all day:
But now I so saucy and churlish am grown,
So ragged and greasy, as never was known;
My Nancy is gone, and my joys are all fled,
And my arse hangs behind me, as heavy as lead.

III

The Kennel, that's wont to run swiftly along,
And dance to soft murmurs dead kittens among,
Thou know'st, little buckhorse, if Nancy was there,
'Twas pleasure to look at, 'twas music to hear:
But now that she's off, I can see it run past,
And still as it murmurs do nothing but blast.
Must you be so cheerful, while I go in pain?
Stop your clack, and be damn'd t'ye, and hear
                              [me complain.

IV

When the bugs in swarms round me wou'd often·
                              [times play,
And Nancy and I were as frisky as they,
We laugh'd at their biting, and kiss'd all the time,
For the spring of her beauty was just in its prime!
But now for their frolics I never can sleep,
So I crack 'em by dozens, as o'er me they creep:
Curse blight you! I cry, while I'm all over smart,
For I'm bit by the arse, while I'm stung to the
                              [heart.

V

The barber I ever was pleased to see,
With his paigtail come scraping to Nancy and me;
And Nancy was pleas'd too, and to the man said,

Come hither, young fellow, and frizzle my head:
But now when he's bowing, I up with my stick,
Cry, blast you, you scoundrel! and give him a kick—
And I'll lend him another, for why should not John
Be as dull as poor Dermot, when Nancy is gone?

VI

When sitting with Nancy, what sights have I seen!
How white was the turnep, the col'wart how green!
What a lovely appearance, while under the shade,
The carrot, the parsnip, the cauliflow'r made!

picks oakum   But now she mills doll, tho' the greens are still there
They none of 'em half so delightful appear:
It was not the board that was nail'd to the wall,
Made so many customers visit our stall.

VII

Sweet music went with us both all the town thro',

[Notes]   To Bagnigge, White Conduit, and Sadler's-Wells
          [too;
Soft murmur'd the Kennels, the beau-pots how
          [sweet,
And crack went the cherry-stones under our feet:

gone   But now she to Bridewell has punch'd it along,
My eye, Betty Martin! on music a song:
'Twas her voice crying mack'rel, as now I have
          [found,
Gave ev'ry-thing else its agreeable sound.

VIII

Gin! What is become of thy heart-chearing fire,
And where is the beauty of Calvert's Intire?
Does aught of its taste Double Gloucester beguile,
That ham, those potatoes, why do they not smile,
Ah! rot ye, I see what it was you were at,
Why you knocked up your froth, why you flash'd
                                      [off your fat:
To roll in her ivory, to pleasure her eye,
To be tipt by her tongue, on her stomach to lie.

IX

How slack is the crop till my Nancy return!
No duds in my pocket, no sea-coal to burn!   money
Methinks if I knew where the watchman wou'd
                                      [tread,
I wou'd follow, and lend him a punch o' the head.
Fly swiftly, good watchman, bring hither my dear,
And, blast me! I'll tip ye a gallon of beer.   treat
Ah, sink him! the watchman is full of delay,
Nor will budge one foot faster for all I can say.

X

Will no blood-hunting foot-pad, that hears me
                                      [complain,
Stop the wind of that nabbing-cull, constable   [Notes]
                          [Payne?

foolish

If he does, he'll to Tyburn next sessions be dragg'd,
And what kiddy's so rum as to get himself
[scragg'd?
No! blinky, discharge her, and let her return;
For ne'er was poor fellow so sadly forlorn.
Zounds! what shall I do? I shall die in a ditch;
Take warning by me how you're leagu'd with a
[bitch.

YE SCAMPS, YE PADS, YE DIVERS [Notes]
[1781]

[From *The Choice of Harlequin*: or *The Indian Chief* by MR. MESSINK, and sung by JOHN EDWIN as "the Keeper of Bridewell"].

I

Ye scamps, ye pads, ye divers, and all upon   footpads; pick
                     [the lay,   pockets;[Notes]
In Tothill-fields gay sheepwalk, like lambs ye sport   Tothill-fields
                  [and play;   prison
Rattling up your darbies, come hither at my call;
I'm jigger dubber here, and you are welcome   warder;
                [to mill doll.   pick oakum
       With my tow row, etc.

II

At your insurance office the flats you've taken in,
The game they've play'd, my kiddy, you're always
               [sure to win;
First you touch the shiners—the number up—   money
               [you break,
With your insuring-policy, I'd not insure your neck.
       With my tow row, etc.

III

feet

The French, with trotters nimble, could fly from
[English blows,

fist

And they've got nimble daddles, as monsieur
[plainly shews;
Be thus the foes of Britain bang'd, ay, thump
[away, monsieur,
The hemp you're beating now will make your
[solitaire.
With my tow row, etc.

IV

eyes

My peepers! who've we here now? why this is
[sure Black-Moll:
My ma'am, you're of the fair sex, so welcome
[to mill doll;

common lodging-
house
[Notes]

The cull with you who'd venture into a snoozing-ken,
Like Blackamore Othello, should "put out the
[light—and then."
With my tow row, etc.

V

I think my flashy coachman, that you'll take better
[care,

drink; abuse

Nor for a little bub come the slang upon your fare;

wig; "footing"

Your jazy pays the garnish, unless the fees you tip,
Though you're a flashy coachman, here the
[gagger holds the whip,
With my tow row, etc.

Chorus omnes

We're scamps, we're pads, we're divers, we're all
                              [upon the lay,
In Tothill-fields gay sheepwalk, like lambs we sport
                              [and play;
Rattling up our darbies, we're hither at your call,
You're jigger dubber here, and we're forc'd for
                              [to mill doll.
            With my tow row, etc.

[Notes]

THE SANDMAN'S WEDDING

[*b.* 1789]

[A Cantata by G. Parker (?)].

Recitative.

As Joe the sandman drove his noble team
Of raw-rump'd jennies, "Sand-ho!" was his theme:

street Just as he turned the corner of the drum,

rag-gatherer His dear lov'd Bess, the bunter, chanc'd to come;

With joy cry'd "Woa", did turn his quid and stare,

kissed her First suck'd her jole, then thus addressed the fair.

Air.

I

Forgive me if I praise those charms

eyes Thy glaziers bright, lips, neck, and arms

Thy snowy bubbies e'er appear
Like two small hills of sand, my dear:
Thy beauties, Bet, from top to toe
Have stole the heart of Sandman Joe.

II

Come wed, my dear, and let's agree,

ale-house Then of the booze-ken you'll be free;

No sneer from cully, mot, or froe follow, girl, or
wife

Dare then reproach my Bess for Joe;

For he's the kiddy rum and queer, brave and cute

That all St. Giles's boys do fear

Recitative.

With daylights flashing, Bess at length reply'd, eyes

Must Joey proffer this, and be deny'd?

No, no, my Joe shall have his heart delight

And we'll be wedded ere we dorse this night; sleep

" Well lipp'd," quoth Joe, " no more you need to spoken

                   [say"—

"Gee-up! gallows, do you want my sand to-day?"

Air.

I

Joe sold his sand, and cly'd his cole, sir, pocketed his
money

    While Bess got a basket of rags,

Then up to St. Giles's they roll'd, sir,

    To every bunter Bess brags:

Then into a booze-ken they pike it, go

    Where Bess was admitted we hear;

For none of the coves dare but like it,

    As Joey, her kiddy, was there.

II

Full of glee, until ten that they started,

    For supper Joe sent out a win;

A hog's maw between them was parted,
    And after they sluic'd it with gin:
It was on an old leather trunk, sir,
    They married were, never to part;
But Bessy, she being blind drunk, sir,
    Joe drove her away in his cart.

THE HAPPY PAIR.   [Notes]

[1789]

[By GEORGE PARKER in *Life's Painter of Variegated Characters*].

Joe.

Ye slang-boys all, since wedlock's nooze,
    Together fast has tied
Moll Blabbermums and rowling Joe,
    Each other's joy and pride;
Your broomsticks and tin kettles bring,   [Notes]
    With cannisters and stones:
Ye butchers bring your cleavers too,
    Likewise your marrow-bones;
For ne'er a brace in marriage hitch'd,
    By no one can be found,
That's half so blest as Joe and Moll,
    Search all St. Giles's round.

Moll.

Though fancy queer-gamm'd smutty Muns
    Was once my fav'rite man,
Though rugged-muzzle tink'ring Tom
    For me left maw-mouth'd Nan:

Though padding Jack and diving Ned,
    With blink-ey'd buzzing Sam,
Have made me drunk with hot, and stood
    The racket for a dram;
Though Scamp the ballad-singing kid,
    Call'd me his darling frow,
I've tip'd them all the double, for
    The sake of rowling Joe.

Chorus.

Therefore, in jolly chorus now,
    Let's chaunt it altogether,
And let each cull's and doxy's heart
    Be lighter than a feather;
And as the kelter runs quite flush,
    Like *natty* shining *kiddies*,
To treat the coaxing, giggling brims,
    With spunk let's post our *neddies*;
Then we'll all roll in *bub* and *grub*,
    Till from this ken we go,
Since rowling Joe's tuck'd up with Moll,
    And Moll's tuck'd up with Joe.

Marginal glosses:
- tramping; pick-pocket
- pickpocket
- paid for
- woman, girl
- jilted
- man; woman
- money
- whores
- spirit; spend our guineas
- drink; food
- drinking-house

THE BUNTER'S CHRISTENING   [Notes]
[1789]

[By GEORGE PARKER in *Life's Painter of Variegated Characters*].

I

Bess Tatter, of Hedge-lane,
   To ragman Joey's joy,
The cull with whom she snooz'd   man
   Brought forth a chopping boy:
Which was, as one might say,
   The moral of his dad, sir;
And at the christ'ning oft,
   A merry bout they had, sir.

II

For, when 'twas four weeks old,
   Long Ned, and dust-cart Chloe,
To give the kid a name,
   Invited were by Joey;
With whom came muzzy Tom,   muddled
   And sneaking Snip, the boozer,   drunkard
Bag-picking, blear-ey'd Ciss,
   And squinting Jack, the bruiser.   pugilist

III

Likewise came bullying Sam,
   With cat's-and-dog's-meat Nelly,
Young Smut, the chimney-sweep,
   And smiling snick-snack Willy;
Peg Swig and Jenny Gog,

harlots; thievish   The brims, with birdlime fingers,
Brought *warbling, seedy* Dick,
   The prince of ballad-singers.

IV

The guests now being met,
   The first thing that was done, sir,
Was handling round the kid,

kiss him   That all might smack his muns, sir;

drop of gin   A *flash of lightning* next,

gave; man;   Bess tipt each cull and frow, sir,
woman
walk   Ere they to church did pad,
   To have it christen'd Joe, sir.

V

Away they then did trudge;
   But such a queer procession,
Of seedy brims and kids,
   Is far beyond expression.

The christ'ning being o'er,
    They back again soon pik't it,   went
To have a dish of lap,   tea
    Prepar'd for those who lik't it.

VI

Bung all come back once more
    They slobber'd little Joey;   kissed
Then, with some civil jaw,   words
    Part squatted, to drink bohea,
And part swig'd barley swipes,   drank beer
    As short-cut they were smoking,   tobacco
While some their patter flash'd   talked
    In gallows fun and joking.   screaming

VII

For supper, Joey stood,
    To treat these curious cronies;
A bullock's melt, hog's maw
    Sheep's heads, and stale polonies:
And then they swill'd gin-hot,
    Until blind drunk as Chloe,
At twelve, all bundled from
    The christ'ning of young Joey.

[Notes] ## THE MASQUERADERS: OR, THE WORLD
AS IT WAGS
[1789]

[By GEORGE PARKER in *Life's Painter of Variegated Characters*].

I

Ye flats, sharps, and rum ones, who make up
[this pother;
Who gape and stare, just like stuck pigs at
[each other,
As mirrors, wherein, at full length do appear,
Your follies reflected so apish and queer
                    Tol de rol, etc.

II

Attend while I *sings*, how, in ev'ry station,
Masquerading is practised throughout ev'ry nation:
Some mask for mere pleasure, but many we know,
money   To lick in the *rhino*, false faces will show.
                    Tol de rol, etc.

III

Twig counsellors jabb'ring 'bout justice and law,
bribing   Cease greasing their fist and they'll soon cease
[their jaw;

And patriots, 'bout freedom will kick up a riot,
Till their ends are all gain'd, and their jaws then
[are quiet.
Tol de rol, etc.

IV

Twig methodist phizzes, with mask sanctimonious, See
Their rigs prove to judge that their phiz is methods
[erroneous.
Twig lank-jaws, the miser, that skin-flint old elf,
From his long meagre phiz, who'd think he'd
[the pelf.
Tol de rol, etc.

V

Twig levées, they're made up of time-*sarving* faces,
With fawning and flatt'ring for int'rest and places;
And ladies appear too at court and elsewhere,
In borrow'd complexions, false shapes, and false hair.
Tol de rol, etc.

VI

Twig clergyman—but as there needs no more proof
My chaunt I *concludes*, and shall now pad the hoof; walk away
So nobles and gents, lug your counterfeits out,
I'll take brums or cut ones, and thank you to boot.
Tol de rol, etc.

[Notes]   THE FLASH MAN OF ST. GILES

[*b.* 1790]

[From *The Busy Bee*].

I

[Notes]   I was a flash man of St. Giles,
And I fell in love with Nelly Stiles;
walked   And I padded the hoof for many miles
To show the strength of my flame:
In the Strand, and at the Admiralty,
victims   She pick'd up the flats as they pass'd by,
stole   handker-
chiefs;   side   And I mill'd their wipes from their side clye,
pocket
And then sung fal de ral tit, tit fal de ral,
Tit fal de ree, and then sung fal de ral tit!

II

girl, whore   The first time I saw the flaming mot,
Was at the sign of the Porter Pot,
I call'd for some purl, and we had it hot,
With gin and bitters too!
talking noisily   We threw off our slang at high and low,
And we were resolv'd to breed a row
[Notes]   For we both got as drunk as David's sow,
And then sung fal de ral tit, etc.

III

As we were roaring forth a catch,
('Twas twelve o'clock) we wak'd the watch,
I at his jazy made a snatch,   wig
And try'd for to nab his rattle!   steal
But I miss'd my aim and down I fell,
And then he charg'd both me and Nell,
And bundled us both to St. Martin's cell
    Where we sung fal de ral tit, etc.

IV

We pass'd the night in love away,
And 'fore justice H— we went next day,
And because we could not three hog pay,   shilling
Why we were sent to quod!   prison
In quod we lay three dismal weeks,
Till Nell with crying swell'd her cheeks,
And I damn'd the quorum all for sneaks
    And then sung fal de ral tit, etc.

V

From Bridewell bars we now are free,
And Nell and I so well agree,
That we live in perfect harmony,
And grub and bub our fill!   eat and drink
For we have mill'd a precious go   made a rich haul
And queer'd the flats at thrums, E, O,

Every night in Titmouse Row,
 Where we sing fal de ral tit, etc.

VI

All you who live at your wit's end,
Unto this maxim pray attend,
Never despair to find a friend,
While flats have bit aboard!
For Nell and I now keep a gig,
And look so grand, so flash and big,
are up to every move We roll in every knowing rig
 While we sing fal de ral tit, etc.

A LEARY MOT

[c. 1811]

[A broadside ballad].

I

Rum old Mog was a leary flash mot, and
    she was round and fat,
With twangs in her shoes, a wheelbarrow too, and
    an oilskin round her hat;
A blue bird's-eye o'er dairies fine—as she mizzled
    through Temple Bar,
Of vich side of the way, I cannot say, but she
    boned it from a Tar—
        Singing, tol-lol-lol-lido.

II

Now Moll's flash com-pan-ion was a Chick-lane
    gill, and he garter'd below his knee,
He had twice been pull'd, and nearly lagg'd,
    but got off by going to sea;
With his pipe and quid, and chaunting voice,
    "Potatoes!" he would cry;
For he valued neither cove nor swell, for he
    had wedge snug in his cly
        Singing, tol-lol-lol-lido.

[Notes]

woman or harlot

Silk-handker-
chief [Notes];
paps; went

stole

sweetheart

gaoled; trans-
ported

money; pocket

III

[Notes]

One night they went to a Cock-and-Hen Club,
    at the sign of the Mare and Stallion,
But such a sight was never seen as Mog and her
    flash com-pan-ion;

kissed

Her covey was an am'rous blade, and he buss'd
    young Bet on the sly,

fist; straight to the spot
rag-gatherer

When Mog up with her daddle, bang-up to the
    mark, and she black'd the Bunter's eye.
Singing, tol-lol-lol-lido.

IV

Now this brought on a general fight, Lord, what

great shindy

    a gallows row—
With whacks and thumps throughout the night,

[Notes]

    till "drunk as David's sow"—

fighting

Milling up and down—with cut heads, and lots
    of broken ribs,
But the lark being over—they ginned themselves
    at jolly Tom Cribb's.
Singing, tol-lol-lol-lido.

"THE NIGHT BEFORE LARRY WAS STRETCHED"

[Notes]

[*c.* 1816]

I

The night before Larry was stretch'd,
    The boys they all paid him a visit;
A bit in their sacks, too, they fetch'd—
    They sweated their duds till they riz it;   pawned their clothes
For Larry was always the lad,
    When a friend was condemn'd to the squeezer,   gallows or rop
But he'd pawn all the togs that he had,   clothes
    Just to help the poor boy to a sneezer,   drink
And moisten his gob 'fore he died.

II

''Pon my conscience, dear Larry', says I,
    'I'm sorry to see you in trouble,
And your life's cheerful noggin run dry,
    And yourself going off like its bubble!'
'Hould your tongue in that matter,' says he;
    'For the neckcloth I don't care a button,   halter
And by this time to-morrow you'll see

Your Larry will be dead as mutton:
   All for what? 'Kase his courage was
        [good!'

III

The boys they came crowding in fast;
   They drew their stools close round about him,
candles   Six glims round his coffin they placed—
   He couldn't be well waked without 'em,
I ax'd if he was fit to die,
   Without having duly repented?
Says Larry, 'That's all in my eye,
   And all by the clargy invented,
     To make a fat bit for themselves.

IV

Then the cards being called for, they play'd,
   Till Larry found one of them cheated;
Quick he made a hard rap at his head—
   The lad being easily heated,
'So ye chates me bekase I'm in grief!
   O! is that, by the Holy, the rason?
Soon I'll give you to know you d—d thief!
   That you're cracking your jokes out of sason,
     And scuttle your nob with my fist'.

V

Then in came the priest with his book
   He spoke him so smooth and so civil;

Larry tipp'd him a Kilmainham look,   [Notes]
    And pitch'd his big wig to the devil.
Then raising a little his head,
    To get a sweet drop of the bottle,
And pitiful sighing he said,
    'O! the hemp will be soon round my throttle,
        And choke my poor windpipe to death!'

VI

So mournful these last words he spoke,
    We all vented our tears in a shower;
For my part, I thought my heart broke
    To see him cut down like a flower!
On his travels we watch'd him next day,
    O, the hangman I thought I could kill him!
Not one word did our poor Larry say,
    Nor chang'd till he came to King William;   [Notes]
    Och, my dear! then his colour turned white.

VII

When he came to the nubbing-cheat,
    He was tack'd up so neat and so pretty;
The rumbler jugg'd off from his feet,   cart
    And he died with his face to the city.
He kick'd too, but that was all pride,
    For soon you might see 'twas all over;
And as soon as the nooze was untied,
    Then at darkey we waked him in clover,   night
        And sent him to take a ground-sweat.   buried him

6

[Notes] # THE SONG OF THE YOUNG PRIG

[*c.* 1819]

I

[Notes]

beggars

My mother she dwelt in Dyot's Isle,
    One of the canting crew, sirs;
And if you'd know my father's style,
    He was the Lord-knows-who, sirs!
I first held horses in the street,
    But being found defaulter,

hackney-coach

Turned rumbler's flunkey for my meat,
    So was brought up to the halter.

pick a pocket; lay
hold of notes or
money
steal handker-
chiefs dextrously
steal a watch;
pocket the plun-
der
steal pocket-
books.

    Frisk the cly, and fork the rag,
      Draw the fogles plummy,
    Speak to the rattles, bag the swag,
      And finely hunt the dummy.

II

My name they say is young Birdlime,
    My fingers are fish-hooks, sirs;

[Notes]

And I my reading learnt betime,
    From studying pocket-books, sirs;

an intended rob-
bery

I have a sweet eye for a plant,

And graceful as I amble,
Finedraw a coat-tail sure I can't
    So kiddy is my famble.   skilful is my hand
    Chorus. Frisk the cly, etc.

III

A night bird oft I'm in the cage,   lock-up
    But my rum-chants ne'er fail, sirs;
The dubsman's senses to engage,   gaoler
    While I tip him leg-bail, sirs;   run away
There's not, for picking, to be had,
    A lad so light and larky,   frolicsome
The cleanest angler on the pad   expert pickpocket
    In daylight or the darkey.   night
    Chorus. Frisk the cly, etc.

IV

And though I don't work capital,   [Notes]
    And do not weigh my weight, sirs;
Who knows but that in time I shall,
    For there's no queering fate, sirs.   getting the better of
If I'm not lagged to Virgin-nee,   transported [Notes]
    I may a Tyburn show be,   be hanged
Perhaps a tip-top cracksman be,   housebreaker
    Or go on the high toby.   become a high-wayman
    Chorus. Frisk the cly, etc.

THE MILLING-MATCH

[1819]

[By THOMAS MOORE in *Tom Crib's Memorial to Congress*:—" Account of the Milling-match between Entellus and Dares, translated from the Fifth Book of the Æneid by One of the Fancy "].

hands; head

With daddles high upraised, and nob held back,
In awful prescience of the impending thwack,

fellows, usually young fellows

Both kiddies stood—and with prelusive spar,
And light manœuvring, kindled up the war!
The One, in bloom of youth—a light-weight
[blade —
The Other, vast, gigantic, as if made,

pugilism

Express, by Nature, for the hammering trade;
But aged, slow, with stiff limbs, tottering much,
And lungs, that lack'd the bellows-mender's touch.

men

Yet, sprightly to the scratch, both Buffers came,
While ribbers rung from each resounding frame,
And divers digs, and many a ponderous pelt,

stomachs

Were on their broad bread-baskets heard and felt.
With roving aim, but aim that rarely miss'd

ears and eyes

Round lugs and ogles flew the frequent fist;

While showers of facers told so deadly well,
That the crush'd jaw-bones crackled as they fell!
But firmly stood Entellus—and still bright,
Though bent by age, with all the Fancy's light,   [Notes]
Stopp'd with a skill, and rallied with a fire
The immortal Fancy could alone inspire!
While Dares, shifting round, with looks of thought.
An opening to the cove's huge carcass sought
(Like General Preston, in that awful hour,
When on one leg he hopp'd to—take the Tower!),
And here, and there, explored with active fin,
And skilful feint, some guardless pass to win,
And prove a boring guest when once let in.

And now Entellus, with an eye that plann'd
Punishing deeds, high raised his heavy hand;
But ere the sledge came down, young Dares spied
Its shadow o'er his brow, and slipped aside—
So nimbly slipp'd, that the vain nobber pass'd
Through empty air; and He, so high, so vast,
Who dealt the stroke, came thundering to the
                              [ground!—
Not B—ck—gh—m himself, with balkier sound,
Uprooted from the field of Whiggist glories,
Fell souse, of late, among the astonish'd Tories!
Instant the ring was broke, and shouts and yells
From Trojan Flashmen and Sicilian Swells
Fill'd the wide heaven--while, touch'd with grief
                              [to see

His pall, well-known through many a lark and spree,

friend ; frolic

heavily Thus rumly floor'd, the kind Ascestes ran,

And pitying rais'd from earth the game old man.

Uncow'd, undamaged to the sport he came,

His limbs all muscle, and his soul all flame.

fighting The memory of his milling glories past,

The shame that aught but death should see him
[grass'd.

All fired the veteran's pluck—with fury flush'd,

Full on his light-limb'd customer he rush'd,—

dealing blows And hammering right and left, with ponderous
[swing

Ruffian'd the reeling youngster round the ring—

Nor rest, nor pause, nor breathing-time was given

But, rapid as the rattling hail from heaven

Beats on the house-top, showers of Randall's shot

Around the Trojan's lugs fell peppering hot!

'Till now Æneas, fill'd with anxious dread,

Rush'd in between them, and, with words well-
[bred,

Preserved alike the peace and Dares' head,

Both which the veteran much inclined to break—

Then kindly thus the punish'd youth bespake:

" Poor Johnny Raw! what madness could impel

So rum a Flat to face so prime a Swell?

See'st thou not, boy, the Fancy, heavenly maid,

Herself descends to this great Hammerer's aid,

And, singling him from all her flash adorers,

Shines in his hits, and thunders in his floorers?
Then, yield thee, youth,—nor such a spooncy be,
To think mere man can mill a Deity!"

Thus spoke the chief—and now, the scrimmage
                                          [o'er,
His faithful pals the done-up Dares bore
Back to his home, with tottering gams, sunk heart,
And muns and noddle pink'd in every part.
While from his gob the guggling claret gush'd   blood
And lots of grinders, from their sockets crush'd   teeth
Forth with the crimson tide in rattling fragments
                                          [rush'd !

YA-HIP, MY HEARTIES!
                    [1819]

[From Moore's *Tom Crib's Memorial to Congress:* —
"Sung by Jack Holmes, the Coachman, at
a late Masquerade in St Giles's, in the
character of Lord C—st—e—on . . . This
song which was written for him by Mr.
Gregson, etc.".]

I

drive a hackney-   I first was hired to *peg* a *Hack*
coach
                    They call "The Erin" sometime back,
talk slang   Where soon I learned to *patter flash*,
horses; whip   To curb the *tits*, and *tip the lash*—
                    Which pleased *the Master of* The Crown
                    So much, he had me up to town,
money   And gave me *lots* of *quids* a year,
drive   To *tool* "The Constitutions" here.
                         So, ya-hip, hearties, here am I
                         That drive the Constitution Fly.

II

Some wonder how the Fly holds out,
So rotten 'tis, within, without;

So loaded too, through thick and thin,
And with such *heavy* creturs IN.
But, Lord, 't will last our time—or if
The wheels should, now and then, get stiff,
Oil of Palm's the thing that, flowing,   money.
Sets the naves and felloes going.
    So ya-hip, *Hearties!* etc.

III

Some wonder, too, the *tits* that pull
This *rum concern* along, so full,
Should never *back* or *bolt*, or kick
The load and driver to Old Nick.
But, never fear, the breed, though British,
Is now no longer *game* or skittish;
Except sometimes about their corn,
Tamer *Houghnhums* ne'er were born.   [Notes]
    So, ya-hip, *Hearties*, etc.

IV

And then so sociably we ride!—
While some have places, snug, inside,
Some hoping to be there anon.
Through many a dirty road *hang on.*
And when we reach a filthy spot
(Plenty of which there are, God wot),
You'd laugh to see with what an air
We *take* the spatter—each his share.
    So, ya-hip, *Hearties*, etc.

SONNETS FOR THE FANCY:

AFTER THE MANNER OF PETRARCH
[*c.* 1824]

[From *Boxiana*, iii. 621. 622].
Education.

A link-boy once, Dick Hellfinch stood the grin,
At Charing Cross he long his toil apply'd;
penny   "Here light, here light! your honours for a win,"
man; woman   To every cull and drab he loudly cried.
In Leicester Fields, as most the story know,
half-penny   "Come black your worship for a single mag,"
spent the money   And while he shin'd his Nelly suck'd the bag,
made a lot of   And thus they sometimes stagg'd a precious go.
money
In Smithfield, too, where graziers' flats resort,
He loiter'd there to take in men of cash,
With cards and dice was up to ev'ry sport,
And at Saltpetre Bank would cut a dash;
cute fellow   A very knowing rig in ev'ry gang,
[i.e. fraternity]   Dick Hellfinch was the pick of all the slang.

Progress.

His Nell sat on Newgate steps, and scratch'd
[her poll,
Her eyes suffus'd with tears, and bung'd
[with gin;

The Session's sentence wrung her to the soul,
　Nor could she lounge the gag to shule a win;
The knowing bench had tipp'd her buzer queer, *sentenced the pick-pocket*
　For Dick had beat the hoof upon the pad,
Of Field, or Chick-lane—was the boldest lad
That ever mill'd the cly, or roll'd the leer. *picked pockets*
　And with Nell he kept a lock, to fence, and tuz,
And while his flaming mot was on the lay,
　With rolling kiddies, Dick would dive and buz,
And cracking kens concluded ev'ry day; *burgling*
　But fortune fickle, ever on the wheel,
　Turn'd up a rubber, for these smarts to feel.

Triumph.

Both'ring the flats assembled round the quod, *goal*
　The queerum queerly smear'd with dirty black; *gallows*
The dolman sounding, while the sheriff's nod,
　Prepare the switcher to dead book the whack,
While in a rattle sit two blowens flash, *coach; women*
　Salt tears fast streaming from each bungy eye;
　To nail the ticker, or to mill the cly *steal a watch; pick a pocket*
Through thick and thin their busy muzzlers splash,
　The mots lament for Tyburn's merry roam,
That bubbl'd prigs must at the New Drop fall, *Newgate*
　And from the start the scamps are cropp'd at
　　　　　　　　　　　　　　　　　[home;
All in the sheriff's picture frame the call *hangman's noose*
　Exalted high, Dick parted with his flame,
　And all his comrades swore that he dy'd game.

[Notes]   # THE TRUE BOTTOM'D BOXER
[1825]

[By J. JONES in *Universal Songster*, ii. 96].

Air: *"Oh! nothing in life can sadden us."*

I

[Notes]   Spring's the boy for a Moulsey-Hurst rig, my lads,
    Shaking a flipper, and milling a pate;
Fibbing a nob is most excellent gig, my lads,
    Kneading the dough is a turn-out in state.
Tapping the claret to him is delighting,
    Belly-go-firsters and clicks of the gob;
For where are such joys to be found as in fighting,
    And measuring mugs for a chancery job:
With flipping and milling, and fobbing and nob-
               [bing,
With belly-go-firsters and kneading the dough,
With tapping of claret, and clipping and gobbing,
    Say just what you please, you must own he's
              the go.

II

Spring's the boy for flooring and flushing it,
    Hitting and stopping, advance and retreat,

For taking and giving, for sparring and rushing it,
And will ne'er say enough, till he's down right
[dead beat;
No crossing for him, true courage and bottom all,
You'll find him a rum un, try on if you can;
You shy-cocks, he shows 'em no favour, 'od rot
['em all,
When he fights he trys to accomplish his man;
With giving and taking, and flooring and flushing,
With hitting and stopping, huzza to the ring,
With chancery suiting, and sparring and rushing,
He's the champion of fame, and of manhood
[the spring.

III

Spring's the boy for rum going and coming it,
Smashing and dashing, and tipping it prime,
Eastward and westward, and sometimes back-
[slumming it,
He's for the scratch, and come up too in time;
For the victualling-office no favor he'll ask it,
For smeller and ogles he feels just the same;
At the pipkin to point, or upset the bread-basket,
He's always in twig, and bang-up for the game;
With going and tipping, and priming and timing
'Till groggy and queery, straight-forwards the rig;
With ogles and smellers, no piping and chiming,
You'll own he's the boy that is always in twig.

[Notes] ## BOBBY AND HIS MARY
[1826]

[From *Universal Songster*, iii. 108].

Tune—*Dulce Domum*.

I

[Notes]: ale-house In Dyot-street a booze-ken stood,
  Oft sought by foot-pads weary,
  And long had been the blest abode
  Of Bobby, and his Mary.
walk around For her he'd nightly pad the hoof,
rob passers-by   And gravel tax collect
  For her he never shammed the snite.
police   Though traps tried to detect him;
  When darkey came he sought his home
girl   While she, distracted blowen
   She hailed his sight,
   And, ev'ry night
   The booze-ken rung
   As they sung,
  O, Bobby and his Mary.

II

  But soon this scene of cozey fuss
  Was changed to prospects queering

The blunt ran shy, and Bobby brush'd,   *money; went off*
    To get more rag not fearing;   *notes or gold*
To Islington he quickly hied,
    A traveller there he dropped on;
The traps were fly, his rig they spied   *object*
    And ruffles soon they popped on.   *handcuffs*
When evening came, he sought not home,
    While she, poor stupid woman,
        Got lushed that night,   *drunk*
        Oh, saw his sprite,
        Then heard the knell
        That bids farewell!
        Then heard the knell
        Of St. Pulchre's bell!   [Notes]
Now he dangles on the Common.

[Notes]

FLASHEY JOE

[1826]

[By R. MORLEY in *Universal Songster*, ii. 194].

I

As Flashey Joe one day did pass
    Through London streets, so jolly,
A crying fish, he spied a lass
    'Twas Tothill's pride, sweet Molly!

mouth ; silk hand-
kerchief [Notes]

He wip'd his mug with bird's-eye blue

kiss

He cried,—" Come, buss your own dear Joe ";
She turned aside, alas! 'tis true
    And bawled out—"Here's live mackerel, O !
        Four a shilling, mackerel, O !
        All alive, O !
        New mackerel, O."

II

talk like that

Says I,—"Miss Moll, don't tip this gam,
    You knows as how it will not do;

fought

For you I milled flash Dustman Sam

eyes

    Who made your peepers black and blue.
Vhy, then you swore you would be kind

acted strangely

    But you have queer'd so much of late,

And always changing like the wind,
    So now I'll brush and sell my skate."   be off
      Buy my skate, etc.

III

She blubb'd—"Now, Joe, vhy treat me ill?
    You know I love you as my life!
When I forsook both Sam and Will,
    And promised to become your wife,
You molled it up with Brick-dust Sall   took as a mistress
    And went to live with her in quod!   gaol
So I'll pike off with my mack'ral   walk
    And you may bolt with your salt cod."
      Here's mack'rel, etc.

IV

I could not part with her, d'ye see
    So I tells Moll to stop her snivel;   crying
"Your panting bubs and glist'ning eye   paps
    Just make me love you like the divil."
"Vhy, then," says she, "come tip's your dad,   shake hands
    And let us take a drap of gin,
And may I choke with hard-roed shad
    If I forsake my Joe Herring."
      Four a shilling, etc.

[Notes]

MY MUGGING MAID
[1826]

[By JAMES BRUTON. *Universal Songster*, iii. 103].

I

[Notes]
ear

Why lie ye in that ditch, so snug,
  With s— and filth bewrayed
With hair all dangling down thy lug
    My mugging maid?

II

tongue

Say, mugging Moll, why that red-rag
  Which oft hath me dismayed,

speech

Why is it now so mute in mag,
    My mugging maid?

III

drink

Why steals the booze down through thy snout,
  With mulberry's blue arrayed,
And why from throat steals hiccough out
    My mugging maid?

IV

mouth

Why is thy mug so wan and blue,
  In mud and muck you're laid;

Say, what's the matter now with you
                    My mugging maid?

V

The flask that in her fam appeared   hand
    The snore her conk betrayed,   nose
Told me, that Hodge's max had queered   [Notes]; got the
                    My mugging maid.   better of

[Notes]

POOR LUDDY

[b. 1826]

[By T. DIBDIN. *Universal Songster*, Vol. iii].

As I was walking down the Strand,
    Luddy, Luddy,
    Ah, poor Luddy, I. O.
As I was walking down the Strand,

police; arrested The traps they nabbed me out of hand
    Luddy, Luddy,
    Ah, poor Luddy, I. O.
        As I was walking, etc.

Said I, kind justice, pardon me,
    Luddy, Luddy,
    Ah, poor Luddy, I. O.
Said I, kind justice, pardon me,
Or Botany-Bay I soon shall see
    Luddy, Luddy,
    Ah, poor Luddy, I. O.
        Said I, kind justice, etc.

Sessions and 'sizes are drawing nigh,
    Luddy, Luddy,
    Ah, poor Luddy, I. O.

Sessions and 'sizes are drawing nigh,
I'd rather you was hung than I.
    Luddy, Luddy,
Ah, poor Luddy, I. O.
        Sessions and 'sizes, etc.

THE PICKPOCKET'S CHAUNT
[1829]

[By W. Maginn: being a translation of Vidocq's song, "En roulant de vergne en vergne "].

I

shop; house

thieving

girl, strumpet, sweetheart

As from ken to ken I was going,
Doing a bit on the prigging lay,
Who should I meet but a jolly blowen,
Tol lol, lol lol, tol dirol lay;
Who should I meet but a jolly blowen,

'cute in business

Who was fly to the time of day.

II

Who should I meet but a jolly blowen,
Who was fly to the time of day,

spoke in slang

I pattered in flash like a covey knowing,
Tol, lol, etc.

drink and food

'Ay, bub or grubby, I say?'

III

I pattered in flash like a covey knowing,
'Ay, bub or grubby, I say?'

'Lots of gatter,' says she, is flowing   porter, beer
    Tol lol, etc.
Lend me a lift in the family way.   [family = frater-
                                    nity of thieves]

IV

Lots of gatter, says she, is flowing
Lend me a lift in the family way.
You may have a crib to stow in.
    Tol lol, etc.
Welcome, my pal, as the flowers in May.

V

You may have a crib to stow in,
Welcome, my pal, as the flowers in May.
To her ken at once I go in
    Tol lol, etc.
Where in a corner out of the way,

VI

To her ken at once I go in.
Where in a corner out of the way
    With his smeller a trumpet blowing   nose
    Tol lol, etc.
A regular swell cove lushy lay.   gentleman; drunk

VII

    With his smeller a trumpet blowing
A regular swell cove lushy lay,

pockets; fingers   To his clies my hooks I throw in
Tol lol, etc.

take his sover-   And collar his dragons clear away.
eigns

VIII

To his clies my hooks I throw in,
And collar his dragons clear away

watch   Then his ticker I set agoing,
Tol lol, etc.

seals   And his onions, chain, and key.

IX

Then his ticker I set a going
And his onions, chain, and key
Next slipt off his bottom clo'ing,
Tol lol, etc.

hat   And his ginger head topper gay.

X

Next slipt off his bottom clo'ing
And his ginger head topper gay.

clothes   Then his other toggery stowing,
Tol lol, etc.

plunder   All with the swag I sneak away.

XI

Then his other toggery stowing
All with the swag I sneak away.

Tramp it, tramp it, my jolly blowen,
 Tol lol, etc.
Or be grabbed by the beaks we may.   taken ; police

XII

Tramp it, tramp it, my jolly blowen
Or be grabbed by the beaks we may.
 And we shall caper a-heel and toeing,
 Tol lol, etc.
A Newgate hornpipe some fine day.   banging

XIII

And we shall caper a-heel and toeing
A Newgate hornpipe some fine day
 With the mots their ogles throwing   girl's; eyes
 Tol lol, etc.
And old Cotton humming his pray.   [Notes]

XIV

With the mots their ogles throwing
And old Cotton humming his pray,
 And the fogle hunters doing
 Tol lol, etc.
Their morning fake in the prigging lay.

[Notes]   ON THE PRIGGING LAY

[1829]

[By H. T. R....: a translation of a French
Slang song ("Un jour à la Croix Rouge")
in Vidocq's *Memoirs*, 1828-9, 4 vols.].

I

pickpockets   Ten or a dozen "cocks of the game,"
thieving game;
thieves' rendez-   On the prigging lay to the flash-house came,
vous
drinking gin;   Lushing blue ruin and heavy wet
porter
evening; sun   Till the darkey, when the downy set.
                           All toddled and begun the hunt
pocket-books;
watches hand-   For readers, tattlers, fogles, or blunt.
kerchiefs; money

II

plunder   Whatever swag we chance for to get,
                             All is fish that comes to net:
                           Mind your eye, and draw the yokel,
                             Don't disturb or use the folk ill.
police   Keep a look out, if the beaks are nigh,
run; before they
see you   And cut your stick, before they're fly.

III

As I vas a crossing St James's Park
I met a swell, a well-togg'd spark.   *well-dressed*
I stops a bit: then toddled quicker,
    For I'd prigged his reader, drawn his ticker;   *stolen his pocket-book and watch*
Then he calls— Stop thief!" thinks I, my master,
    That's a hint to me to mizzle faster.   *run*

IV

When twelve bells chimed, the prigs returned,   *thieves*
    And rapped at the ken of Uncle ——:   *house*
" Uncle, open the door of your crib
    If you'd share the swag, or have one dib.   *plunder; coin*
Quickly draw the bolt of your ken,
    Or we'll not shell out a mag, old ——."   *give you a half-penny*

V

Then says Uncle, says he, to his blowen,   *woman*
    " D'ye twig these coves, my mot so knowing?   *known; men; mistress;*
Are they out-and-outers, dearie?   *safe to trust*
    Are they fogle-hunters, or cracksmen leary?   *pickpockets; burglars*
Are they coves of the ken, d'ye know?   *of our band*
    Shall I let 'em in, or tell 'em to go?"

VI

" Oh! I knows 'em now; hand over my breeches—
    I always look out for business—vich is

A reason vy a man should rouse
At any hour for the good of his house.
a cheery greeting The top o' the morning, gemmen all,
And for vot you vants, I begs you'll call."

VII

police But now the beaks are on the scene,
And watched by moonlight where we went;—
saw us going Stagged us a toddling into the ken,
And were down upon us all; and then
dandy Who should I spy but the slap-up spark
robbed of the plunder What I eased of the swag in St James's Park.

VIII

There's a time, says King Sol, to dance and
[sing;
I know there's a time for another thing:
There's a time to pipe, and a time to snivel—
police and magistrates I wish all Charlies and beaks at the divel:
For they grabbed me on the prigging lay,
transported And I know I'm booked for Bot'ny Bay.

THE LAG'S LAMENT   [Notes]

[1829]

[By H. T. R. in *Vidocq's Memoirs*, Vol III. 169].

I

Happy the days when I vorked away,
  In my usual line in the prigging lay,   picking pockets
Making from this, and that, and t'other,
  A tidy living without any bother:
When my little crib was stored with swag,   plunder
  And my cly vas a vell-lined money bag,   pocket
Jolly vas I, for I feared no evil,
  Funked at naught, and pitched care to the devil.

II

I had, beside my blunt, my blowen,   money; mistress
  'So gay, so nutty and so knowing'   [Notes]
On the wery best of grub we lived,   food
  And sixpence a quartern for gin I gived;
My toggs was the sportingst blunt could buy,   clothes; money
  And a slap-up out-and-outer was I.
Vith my mot on my arm, and my tile on my head,   hat
  'That ere's a gemman' every von said.

III

A-coming avay from Wauxhall von night,
drunken   I cleared out a muzzy cove quite;
He'd been a strutting avay like a king,
And on his digit he sported a ring,
A di'mond sparkler, flash and knowing,
    Thinks I, I'll vatch the vay he's going,
And fleece my gemman neat and clever,
    So, at least I'll try my best endeavour.

IV

A'ter, the singing and fire-vorks vas ended,
    I follows my gemman the vay he tended
In a dark corner I trips up his heels,
watch; pocket-book   Then for his tattler and reader I feels,
pockets his money I pouches his blunt, and I draws his ring,
    Prigged his buckles and every thing,
And saying, "I thinks as you can't follow, man,"
ran off   I pikes me off to Ikey Soloman.

V

Then it happened, d'ye see, that my mot,
    Yellow a-bit about the swag that I'd got,
Thinking that I should jeer and laugh,
indulge in banter Although I never tips no chaff
Tries her hand at the downy trick,
    And prigs in a shop, but precious quick

" Stop thief! " was the cry, and she vas taken
I cuts and runs and saves my bacon.

VI

" Then," says he, says Sir Richard Birnie,   [Notes]
    " I adwise you to nose on your pals, and turn the   inform
Snitch on the gang, that'll be the best vay   betray
    To save your scrag." Then, without delay,   neck
He so prewailed on the treach'rous varmint
    That she was noodled by the Bow St. sarmint   persuaded
Then the beaks they grabbed me, and to prison   police ; arrested
                        [I vas dragged
And for fourteen years of my life I vas lagged.   transported

VII

My mot must now be growing old,
    And so am I if the truth be told;
But the only vay to get on in the vorld,
    Is to go with the stream, and however ve're
To bear all rubs; and ven ve suffer   [twirld,
    To hope for the smooth ven ve feels the rougher,
Though very hard, I confess it appears,
    To be lagged, for a lark, for fourteen years.

"NIX MY DOLL, PALS, FAKE AWAY"

[1834]

[Notes]

[By W. HARRISON AINSWORTH, being Jerry Juniper's chaunt in *Rookwood*].

cell; Newgate In a box of the stone jug I was born,
woman whose
husband has Of a hempen widow the kid forlorn,
been hanged;
child   Fake away!
work away!
And my father, as I've heard say,
Fake away!

dancing master Was a merchant of capers gay,
Who cut his last fling with great applause.

never mind, Nix my doll, pals, fake away!
friends
hanging To the time of hearty choke with caper sauce.
Fake away!

thieves; prison The knucks in quod did my schoolmen play,
Fake away!

taught me thiev- And put me up to the time of day,
ing
Until at last there was none so knowing,

shoplifter; pick- No such sneaksman or buzgloak going,
pocket
Fake away!

silk bandker- Fogles and fawnies soon went their way,
chiefs; rings
Fake away!

To the spout with the sneezers in grand array,   pawnbrokers ; snuffboxes

No dummy hunter had forks so fly,   pocket-book ; nimble fingers

No knuckler so deftly, could fake a cly,   pickpocket: steal

Fake away!

No slourd hoxter my snipes could stay,   inside pocket buttoned up

Fake away!

None knap a reader like me in the lay.   steal a pocket-book

Soon then I mounted in swell street-high,

Nix my doll, pals, fake away!

Soon then I mounted in swell street-high.

And sported my flashest toggery,   best made clothes

Fake away!

Fainly resolved I would make my hay,

Fake away!

While Mercury's star shed a single ray;

And ne'er was there seen such a dashing prig,

With my strummel faked in the newest twig,   hair dressed ; fashion

Fake away!

With my fawnied famms and my onions gay,   hands bejewelled ; seals

Fake away!

My thimble of ridge and my driz kemesa,   gold watch ; lace-frilled shirt

All my togs were so niblike and plash.   clothes; fashionable ; fine

Readily the queer screens I then could smash.   forged notes ; pass

Fake away!

But my nuttiest blowen one fine day,   favorite girl

Fake away!

To the beaks did her fancy-man betray,   magistrates; sweetheart

Aud thus was I bowled at last,

8

And into the jug for a lag was cast,
    Fake away!
handcuffs   But I slipped my darbies one morn in May,
warder   And gave to the dubsman a holiday,
And here I am, pals, merry and free,
gypsy   A regular rollicking romany.

THE GAME OF HIGH TOBY   [Notes]
[1834]

[By W. HARRISON AINSWORTH in *Rookwood*].

I

Now Oliver puts his black night-cap on,   the moon
  And every star its glim is hiding,   light
And forth to the heath is the scampsman gone,   highwayman
  His matchless cherry-black prancer riding;   black horse
Merrily over the Common he flies,
  Fast and free as the rush of rocket,
His crape-covered vizard drawn over his eyes,
  His tol by his side and his pops in his pocket.   sword; pistols

Chorus.
    Then who can name
    So merry a game,
As the game of all games—high-toby?   high-way robbery

II

The traveller hears him, away! away!
  Over the wide, wide heath he scurries;
He heeds not the thunderbolt summons to stay,
  But ever the faster and faster he hurries,

fleet horse; horse   But what daisy-cutter can match that black tit?
                              He is caught—he must 'stand and deliver';
pocket book   Then out with the dummy, and off with the bit,
                              Oh! the game of high-toby for ever!

Chorus.

Then who can name
So merry a game
As the game of all games—high-toby?

III

Believe me, there is not a game, my brave boys,
    To compare with the game of high-toby;
highwayman   No rapture can equal the tobyman's joys,
bullets   To blue devils, blue plumbs give the go-by;
gallows   And what if, at length, boys, he come to the crap!
    Even rack punch has *some* bitter in it,
gallows   For the mare-with-three-legs, boys, I care not
                                   [a rap,
'Twill be over in less than a minute!

Chorus.

Then hip, hurrah!
Fling care away!
Hurrah for the game of high-toby!

THE DOUBLE CROSS [Notes]
[1834]

[By W. HARRISON AINSWORTH, in *Rookwood*].

I

Though all of us have heard of crost fights,
And certain gains, by certain lost fights;
I rather fancies that its news,
How in a mill, both men should lose;   fight
For vere the odds are thus made even,
It plays the dickens with the steven: money
Besides, against all rule they're sinning,
Vere neither has no chance of vinning.
            Ri, tol, lol, etc.

II

Two milling coves, each vide awake,
Vere backed to fight for heavy stake;
But in the mean time, so it vos,
Both kids agreed to play a cross;
Bold came each buffer to the scratch,   man
To make it look a tightish match;
They peeled in style, and bets were making,   stripped

'Tvos six to four, but few were taking.

                Ri, tol, lol, etc.

III

Quite cautiously the mill began,
For neither knew the other's plan :
Each cull completely in the dark,
Of vot might be his neighbour's mark;
Resolved his fibbing not to mind,
Nor yet to pay him back in kind;
So on each other kept they tout,
And sparred a bit, and dodged about.

                Ri, tol, lol, etc.

fellow

[Notes]

IV

Vith mawleys raised, Tom bent his back,
As if to place a heavy thwack;
Vile Jem, with neat left handed stopper,
Straight threatened Tommy with a topper;
'Tis all my eye! no claret flows,
No facers sound—no smashing blows,
Five minutes pass, yet not a hit,
How can it end, pals?— vait a bit.

                Ri, tol, lol, etc.

hands

blood

V

Each cove vos teared with double duty,
To please his backers, yet play booty,

deceive them

Ven, luckily for Jem, a teller
Vos planted right upon his smeller   nose
Down dropped he, stunned; ven time was called
Seconds in vain the seconds bawled;
The mill is o'er, the crosser crost,
The losers von, the vinners lost.

[Notes]

THE THIEVES' CHAUNT
[1836]

(By W. H. SMITH in *The Individual*).

I

public house   There is a nook in the boozing ken,
pipe ; smoke   Where many a mug I fog,
And the smoke curls gently, while cousin Ben
Keeps filling the pots again and again,
paid a shilling   If the coves have stump'd their hog.

II

The liquors around are diamond bright,
gin   And the diddle is best of all;
But I never in liquors took delight,
humbug   For liquors I think is all a bite,
porter   So for heavy wet I call.

III

The heavy wet in a pewter quart,
As brown as a badger's hue,
sherry   More than Bristol milk or gin,
Brandy or rum, I tipple in,
mistress   With my darling blowen, Sue.

IV

Oh! grunting peck in its eating *pork*
Is a richly soft and savoury thing;
A Norfolk capon is jolly grub *red-herring*
When you wash it down with strength of bub: *lots of beer*
But dearer to me Sue's kisses far,
Than grunting peck or other grub are,
And I never funks the lambskin men, *judges*
When I sits with her in the boozing ken.

V

Her duds are bob—she's a kinchin crack, *clothes; neat; fine young woman*
And I hopes as how she'll never back;
For she never lushes dog's-soup or lap, *drinks water or tea*
But she loves my cousin the bluffer's tap. *inn-keeper*
She's wide-awake, and her prating cheat, *tongue*
For humming a cove was never beat; *fooling a man*
But because she lately nimm'd some tin, *stole; money*
They have sent her to lodge at the King's Head Inn. *Newgate [Notes]*

THE HOUSE BREAKER'S SONG
[*c.* 1838]

[By G. W. M. REYNOLDS in *Pickwick Abroad*].

I

police spy; share of the booty
house was burgled

gentlemanly

police-officers

Old Bailey pleaders
prison
gunpowder, hand dextrous at thieving
thieves

double-barrelled gun

I ne'er was a nose, for the reg'lars came
Whenever a pannie was done:—
Oh! who would chirp to dishonour his name,
And betrays his pals in a nibsome game
To the traps?—Not I for one!
Let nobs in the fur trade hold their jaw,
And let the jug be free:—
Let Davy's dust and a well-faked claw
For fancy coves be the only law,
And a double-tongued squib to keep in awe
The chaps that flout at me!

II

drink freely

brandy

depart

From morn till night we'll booze a ken,
And we'll pass the bingo round;
At dusk we'll make our lucky, and then,
With our nags so fresh, and our merry men,
We'll scour the lonely ground.
And if the swell resist our "Stand!"

We'll squib without a joke; *fire*
For I'm snigger'd if we will be trepanned *transported*
By the blarneying jaw of a knowing hand,
And thus be lagged to a foreign land,
    Or die by an artichoke. *hanging [hearty choke]*

III

But should the traps be on the sly,
    For a change we'll have a crack; *burglary*
The richest cribs shall our wants supply— *houses*
Or we'll knap a fogle with fingers fly, *steal; handker-chief*
    When the swell one turns his back. *skilful*
The flimsies we can smash as well, *pass false notes*
    Or a ticker deftly prig:— *watch*
But if ever a pal in limbo fell, *prison*
He'd sooner be scragg'd at once than tell; *hanged*
Though the hum-box patterer talked of hell, *parson*
    And the beak wore his nattiest wig. *magistrate; handsomest*

[Notes] ## "THE FAKING BOY TO THE CRAP
IS GONE"

[1841]

[By BON GAULTIER in *Tait's Edinburgh Magazine*].

I

pickpocket; gal-
lows

gallows

The faking boy to the crap is gone,
At the nubbing-cheat you'll find him;
The hempen cord they have girded on,
And his elbows pinned behind him.

blast my eyes!

"Smash my glim," cries the reg'lar card,
"Though the girl you love betrays you,
Don't split, but die both game and hard,
And grateful pals shall praise you."

II

The bolt it fell,—a jerk, a strain!
The sheriff's fled asunder;
The faking-boy ne'er spoke again,
For they pulled his legs from under.
And there he dangles on the tree,
That sort of love and bravery!
Oh, that such men should victims be
Of law, and law's vile knavery.

THE NUTTY BLOWEN   [Notes]
[1841]

[By Bon Gaultier in *Tait's Edinburgh Magazine*].

I

She wore a rouge like roses, the night when
    first we met,
Her lovely mug was smiling o'er mugs of heavy   face;
    wet;   porter
Her red lips had the fullness, her voice the
    husky tone,
That told her drink was of a kind where water
    is unknown.
I saw her but a moment, yet methinks I see
    her now,
With the bloom of borrowed flowers upon her
    cheek and brow.

II

A pair of iron darbies, when next we met,   handcuffs
    she wore,
The expression of her features was more thoughtful
    than before ;
And, standing by her side, was he who strove
    with might and main

To soothe her leaving that dear land she ne'er
    might see again.
I saw her but a moment, yet methinks I see
    her now,
As she dropped the judge a curtsey, and he
    made her a bow.

III

And once again I see that brow no idle rouge
    is there,

gaoler's

The dubsman's ruthless hand has cropped her
    once luxurious hair;
She teases hemp in solitude, and there is no
    one near,
To press her hand within his own, and call for
    ginger-beer.
I saw her but a moment, yet methinks I see
    her now,
With the card and heckle in her hand, a-teas-
    ing of that tow.

THE FAKER'S NEW TOAST   [Notes]
[1841]

[By Bon Gaultier ("Nimming Ned") in *Tait's Edinburgh Magazine*]

I

Come, all ye jolly covies, vot faking do admire,   fellows; stealing
And pledge them British authors who to our line
    aspire ;
Who, if they were not gemmen born, like us
    had kicked at trade,
And every one had turned him out a genuine
    fancy blade,   pickpocket
            And a trump.

II

'Tis them's the boys as knows the vorld, 'tis them
    as knows mankind,
And vould have picked his pocket too, if Fortune
    (vot is blind)
Had not to spite their genius, stuck them in a
    false position,
Vere they can only write about, not execute their
    mission,
            Like a trump.

If they goes on as they're begun, things soon will
    come about,
And ve shall be the upper class, and turn the
    others out;
Their laws ve'll execute ourselves, and raise their
    hevelation,
That's tit for tat, for they'd make that the only
    recreation
                                    Of a trump.

IV

But ketch us! only vait a bit, and ve shall be
    their betters;
For vitch our varmest thanks is due unto the
    men of letters,
Who, good 'uns all, have showed us up in our
    own proper light,
steal   And proved ve prigs for glory, and all becos
    it's right
                                    In a trump.

V

'Tis ve as sets the fashion: Jack Sheppard is
fashion   the go
And every word of 'Nix my dolls' the finest
    ladies know;

And ven a man his vortin'd make, vy, vot d'ye
   think's his vay?
He does vot ve vere used to do—he goes to
   Botany Bay   [Notes]
                   Like a trump.

VI

Then fill your glasses, dolly palls, vy should they
   be neglected,
As does their best to helewate the line as ve's
   selected?
To them as makes the Crackman's life, the burglar's
   subject of their story,
To Ainsworth, and to Bullvig, and to Reynolds [Notes]
   be the glory,
                  Jolly trumps.

[Notes]

MY MOTHER

[1841]

[By Bon Gaultier in *Tait's Edinburgh Magazine*].

I

Who, when a baby, lank and thin,
I called for pap and made a din,
Lulled me with draughts of British gin?—

> My mother.

II

When I've been out upon the spree,
And not come home till two or three,
Who was it then would wallop me?—

> My mother.

III

well-dressed man Who, when she met a heavy swell,
handkerchief Would ease him of his wipe so well,
And kiss me not to go and tell?—

> My mother.

IV

Who took me from my infant play,
And taught me how to fake away.

And put me up to the time of day?—   made me cunning
> My mother.

V

Who'd watch me sleeping in my chair,
And slily to my fob repair,   pocket
And leave me not a mopus there?—   penny
> My mother.

VI

Who, as beneath her care I grew,
Taught my young mind a thing or two,
Especially the flats to do?—   stupid ones
> My mother.

VII

I'm blessed if ever I did see,
So regular a trump as she:
I own my virtues all to thee,—
> My mother.

VIII

So hand, my pals, the drink about,
My story and my glass are out,
A bumper, boys, and with me shout—
> My mother.

THE HIGH-PADS FROLIC
[1841]

[By LEMAN REDE, being Kit's and Adelgitha's Duet in *Sixteen String Jack*].

I

Ade. Crissy odsbuds, I'll on with my duds,
   And over the water we'll flare;

Kit. Coaches and prads, lasses and lads,
   And fiddlers will be there.

Ade. There beauty blushes bright,
Kit.   The punch is hot and strong,
Both. {And there we'll whisk it, frisk it, whisk it,
   { Skip it, and trip it along!

II

Ade. There's Charley Rattan, and natty Jack
   And giant-like Giles McGhee;   [Rann,
   There's Sidle so slim, and flare-away Tim,
   And all of them doat on me.
Kit.   Hadelgitha—platonically, Christopher!
Ade. But Charley, and Jack, and Tim,
   In vain may exert their wit.

For still I'll dance it, prance it, dance it,
Flaring away with Kit!

II

Kit.   There's frollicking Kate, and rollicking Bet,
    And slammerkin Sall so tall,
  And leary-eyed Poll, and blue-eyed Moll—
    Blow me, I love them all!
      Christopher—platonically, Hadelgitha!
  But Winny, not Jenny, nor Sue,
    Shall wean this heart from thee—
  So thus I'll trip it, lip it, trip it,
    Trip it with Hadelgitha!

IV

Kit.   The morning may dawn as sure as you're
Ade.   Will find us dancing alone   [born,
Kit.   I'll get a hack, be off in a crack,   instant
Ade.   An elegant Darby and Joan!
    How'll the vulgarians stare
      As they see you sportingly!
    For none can splash it, dash it, splash it,
Both.   Crissy
      Addy   little you and I.

THE DASHY, SPLASHY....
LITTLE STRINGER

[1841]

[By LEMAN REDE, being Kit's Song in *Sixteen-String Jack*].

I

A cloudy night, and pretty hard it blow'd,

spirited horse   The dashy, splashy, leary little stringer,

Mounted his roan, and took the road—

                        Phililoo!

"My Lord Cashall's on the road to-night,

Down with the lads, make my lord alight—

Ran dan row de dow, on we go!"

        Chorus.—Ran, dan, etc.

II

"You horrid wretch," said my Lord to Rann—

The dashy, splashy, leary little stringer—

"How dare you rob a gentleman?"

                        Phililoo!

wink   Says Jack, says he, with his knowing phiz,

"I ain't very pertic'lar who it is!

Ran dan row de dow, on we go!"

        Chorus.—Ran, dan, etc.

III

Ve collar'd the blunt, started off for town,   money
  With the dashy, splashy, leary little stringer,
Horses knock'd up, men knock'd down—
                 Phililoo!
A lady's carriage we next espied,
I collar'd the blunt, Jack jumped inside,
  Ran dan row de dow, on we go!
      Chorus.—Ran, dan, etc.

IV

Jack took off his hat, with a jaunty air—
  The dashy, splashy, leary little stringer—
And he kiss'd the lips of the lady fair—
                 Phililoo!
She sigh'd a sigh, and her looks said plain,
I don't care much if I'm robb'd again!
  Ran dan row de dow, on we go!
      Chorus.—Ran, dan, etc.

THE BOULD YEOMAN
[1842]

[By PIERCE EGAN in *Captain Macheath*].

I

tell·highwayman A chant I'll tip to you about a High-pad pal
    so down,
pistols: horse With his pops, and high-bred prad which brought
    to him renown;
On the road he cut a dash, to him 'twas delight!
men And if culls would not surrender, he shewed the
    kiddies fight!
    With his pops so bright and airy,
    And his prad just like a fairy,
steal   He went out to nab the gold!
    Derry down, down, derry down,

II

He met a bould yeoman, and bid him for to stand;
" If I do, I'm damn'd! " said he, " although you
    cut it grand.
I'm an old English farmer, and do not me provoke
I've a cudgel, look ye here, it's a prime tough
    bit of oak!

And I'll give you some gravy,   beating
Of that I'll take my davy,   oath
If you try to prig my gold   steal
    Derry down.

III

Then the High-toby gloque drew his cutlass so [Notes]
    fine;
Says he to the farmer, "you or I for the shine!"
And to it they went both, like two Grecians of old,
Cutting, slashing, up and down, and all for the gold!
    'Twas cut for cut while it did last,
    Thrashing, licking, hard and fast,
    Hard milling for the gold.   fighting
        Derry down.

IV

The High-pad quickly cut the farmer's towel in cudgel
    twain—
Pulled out his barking-iron to send daylight through pistol; shoot him
    his brain;
But said he I will not down you, if you will but
    disburse
Your rowdy with me, yeoman—I'm content to money
    whack your purse!
    Down with the dust, and save your life, money
    Your consent will end our strife,
    Ain't your life worth more than gold?
        Derry down.

V

money   Hand up the pewter, farmer, you shall have a
         share

         A kindness, for a toby gloque, you must say is rare;

money   That's right—tip up the kelter, it will make my
         bones amends,

         And wherever we may meet, farmer, we'll be
         the best of friends!

horse   So mount your trotter and away,
          And if you ever come this way,
          Take better care of your gold!
          Derry down.

VI

         Now listen to me, lads, and always you'll do well,

pocket   Empty every clie of duke, commoner, or swell;

brave man   But if you stop a game cove, who has little else
         than pluck,

rob him of all   Do not clean him out, and you'll never want
         for luck.

         So High-pads drink my toast,
         Let honour be our boast,
         And never pluck a poor cull of his gold.
         Derry down.

THE BRIDLE-CULL AND HIS LITTLE POP-GUN

[Notes]

[1842]

[By PIERCE EGAN in *Captain Macheath*].

I

My brave brother troopers, slap-up in the abode,
Come listen unto me while I chant about " the
    Road";
Oh prick up your list'ners if you are fond of fun   ears
A bridle-cull's the hero, and his little pop-gun.   highwayman
    Fal, de, rol! lal! lal! la!

II

One morning early he went, this rollicking blade,   fellow
To pick the blunt up, and he met a nice young   money
    maid;
" I'll not rob you," said he, "and so you needn't
    bunk;"   run away
But she lammas'd off in style, of his pop-gun   went off;
    Fal, de, rol! lal! lal! la!   [afunk.   afraid

III

Then up came a stage-coach, and thus the
    gloque did say,   highwayman

I'm sorry for to stop you, but you must hear
    my lay;
"Come, stand and deliver! if not, sure as the sun,
Your journey I will stop with my little pop-gun."
       Fal, de, rol! lol! lol!

IV

highwayman

money

'Tis by these little lays a High-padsman he thrives,
"Oh take all our rhino, but pray spare our lives!"
Cry the passengers who anxious all are for to run,
Frightened nigh to death by his little pop-gun."
       Fol, de, rol.

V

companions; out
of luck;
plunder

watches; money;
transportation

talk; civilly; give

money

Then, my blades, when you're bush'd, and must
    have the swag,
Walk into tattlers, shiners, and never fear the lag;
Then patter to all spicey, and tip 'em lots of fun,
And blunt you'll never want while you've got a
    pop-gun.
       Fol, de, rol! la!

JACK FLASHMAN

[1842]

[By PIERCE EGAN in *Captain Macheath*].

I

Jack Flashman was a prig so bold,
Who sighed for nothen but the gold;
For sounding, frisking any clie,   *robbing; pocket*
Jack was the lad, and never shy.
      Fol, de, rol.

II

Jack long was on the town, a teazer;   *clever fellow*
A spicy blade for wedge or sneezer;   *silver plate; snuffbox*
Could turn his fives to anything   *hands*
Nap a reader, or filch a ring.   *pocket-book; steal a ring*
      Fol, de, rol.

III

Jack was all game, and never slack,   *bold*
In the darky tried the crack;   *evening; burglary*
Frisk'd the lobby and the swag;
"I'm fly to every move," his brag.   *aware of*
      Fol, de, rol.

IV

But Jack, at last, got too knowen—

betrayed by his mistress   Was made a flat by his blowen!

gave information   She peached, so got him into trouble.

deserted   And then, tipp'd poor Jack the double!

           Fol, de, rol.

V

prison   Jack left the jug right mer-ri-ly,

sweetheart   And vent and black'd his doxy's eye!

Saying—look, marm, when next you split,

I'll finish you with a rummy hit!

           Fol, de, rol.

VI

men   My blades, before my chaunt I end,

advice   Here the rag-sauce of a friend;

Ne'er trust to any fancy jade,

For all their chaff is only trade!

           Fol, de, rol.

VII

Let all their gammon be resisted;

hung   Vithout you vishes to get twisted!

talk about   And never nose upon yourself—

You then are sure to keep your pelf.

           Fol, de, riddle.

MISS DOLLY TRULL

[1842]

[Notes]

[By PIERCE EGAN in *Captain Macheath*].

I

Of all the mots in this here jug,   women; prison
  There's none like saucy Dolly;
And but to view her dimber mug   pretty face
  Is e'er excuse for folly.
She runs such precious cranky rigs
  With pinching wedge and lockets   stealing plate
Yet she's the toast of all the prigs
  Though stealing hearts and pockets.

II

Just twig Miss Dolly at a hop—   see; dance
  She tries to come the graces!   act
To gain her end she will not stop
  And all the swells she chases.
She ogles, nods, and patters flash   talks slang
  To ev'ry flatty cully   susceptible fellow
Until she frisks him, at a splash   robs; entirely
  Of rhino, wedge, and tully.   money

[Notes]

THE BY-BLOW OF THE JUG
[1842]

[By Pierce Egan in *Captain Macheath*].

I

child

In Newgate jail the jolly kid was born—
Infamy he suck'd without any scorn!
His mammy his father did not know,
But that's no odds—Jack was a by-blow!
Foddy, loddy, high O.

II

feet

Scarcely had Jack got on his young pins,
When his mammy put him up to some very
[bad sins,
And she taught him soon to swear and lie,
And to have a finger in every pie.
Foddy, loddy, high O.

III

accomplished;

thief

round for theft

His mammy was downy to every rig,—
Before he could read she made him a prig;
Very soon she larn'd Jack to make a speak
And he toddled out on the morning sneak
Foddy, loddy, high O.

IV

Jack had a sharp-looking eye to ogle,   leer
And soon he began to nap the fogle!   steal; handker-
                   chief
And ever anxious to get his whack—
When scarcely ripe, he went on the crack. housebreaking
   Foddy, loddy, high O.

V

" Now, my chick," says she, "you must take the
'Tis richer than the finest abode,   [road!
For watches, purses, and lots of the gold—
A scampsman, you know, must always be bold." highwayman
   Foddy, loddy, high O.

VI

His mother then did give Jack some advice,
To her son a thief, who was not o'er nice;
Says she—" Fight your way, Jack, and stand the
            [brunt,
You're of no use, my child, without the blunt, money
   Foddy, loddy, high O.

VII

"Then keep it up, Jack, with rare lots of fun.
A short life, perhaps, but a merry one;
Your highway dodges may then live in fame,

Cheat miss-Fortune, and be sure to die game."
        Foddy, loddy, high O.

VIII

"In spite of bad luck, don't be a grumbler;
cart [Notes]   If you are finished off from a tumbler!
But to the end of your life, cut a shine,
You're not the first man got into a line."
        Foddy, loddy, high O.

THE CADGER'S BALL   [Notes]
[1852]

[From JOHN LABERN'S *Popular Comic Song Book*].

Tune—*Joe Buggins*.

I

Oh, what a spicy flare-up, tear-up,
    Festival Terpsickory,
Was guv'd by the genteel cadgers
    In the famous Rookery.
As soon as it got vind, however,
    Old St Giles's vos to fall—
They all declar'd, so help their never,
    They'd vind up vith a stunnin' ball!
        Tol, lol lol, etc.

II

Jack Flipflap took the affair in hand, sirs—
    Who understood the thing complete—
He'd often danced afore the public,
    On the boards, about the streets.
Old Mother Swankey, she consented
    To lend her lodging-house for nix—   nothing

Say's she, 'The crib comes down to-morrow,

merrily   So, go it, just like beans and bricks.'

Tol, lol lol, etc.

III

walking   The night arrived for trotter-shaking—

lodging-house   To Mother Swankey's snoozing-crib;

Each downy cadger was seen taking

sweetheart; wife   His bit of muslin, or his rib.

Twelve candles vos stuck into turnips,

Suspended from the ceiling queer—

Bunn's blaze of triumph was all pickles

To this wegetable shandileer.

Tol, lol lol, etc.

IV

Ragged Jack, wot chalks 'Starvation !'

Look'd quite fat and swellish there—

While Dick, wot 'dumbs it' round the nation,

Had all the jaw among the fair.

Limping Ned wot brought his duchess,

At home had left his wooden pegs—

And Jim, wot cadges it on crutches,

Vos the nimblest covey on his legs.

Tol, lol lol, etc.

V

The next arrival was old Joe Burn,

Wot does the fits to Natur chuff—

And Fogg, wot's blind each day in Ho'born,
   Saw'd his way there clear enough,
Mr. Sinniwating Sparrow,
   In corduroys span new and nice,
Druv up in his pine-apple barrow,
   Which he used to sell a win a slice.   penny
        Tol, lol lol, etc.

VI

The ball was open'd by fat Mary,
   Togg'd out in book muslin pure,   dressed
And Saucy Sam, surnamed 'The Lary,'
   Who did the '*Minuit-on-a-squre.*'
While Spifflicating Charley Coker,
   And Jane of the Hatchet-face divine,
Just did the Rowdydowdy Poker,
   And out of Greasy took the shine.   [Grisi?]
        Tol, lol lol, etc.

VII

The Sillywarious next was done in
   Tip-top style just as it should,
By Muster and Missus Mudfog, stunning,
   Whose hair curled like a bunch of wood.
The folks grinn'd all about their faces,
   'Cos Mudfog—prince of flashy bucks—
Had on a pair of pillow Cases,
   Transmogrified slap into ducks!
        Tol, lol lol, etc.

VIII

The celebrated Pass de Sandwich
     To join in no one could refuse—
Six bushels on 'em came in, and wich
     Wanish'd in about two two's.
beer   The Gatter Waltz next followed arter—
drunk   They lapp'd it down, right manful-ly,
Until Joe Guffin and his darter,
     Was in a state of Fourpen-ny!
               Tol, lol lol, etc.

IX

Next came the Pass de Fascination
     Betwixt Peg Price and Dumby Dick—
But Peg had sich a corporation,
     He dropp'd her like a red hot brick.
The company was so enraptur'd,
     They *buckets* of vall flowers threw—
But one chap flung a bunch of turnips,
     Which nearly split Dick's nut in two.
               Tol, lol lol, etc.

X

The dose now set to gallopading,
     And stamp'd with all their might and main--
They thump'd the floor so precious hard-in,
house   It split the ancient crib in twain,

Some pitch'd in the road, bent double—
  Some was smash'd with bricks—done brown—
So the cadgers saved 'The Crown' the trouble
  Of sending coves to pull it down.
         Tol, lol lol, etc.

"DEAR BILL, THIS STONE-JUG"

[1857]

[From *Punch*, 31 Jan., p. 49. Being an Epistle from
Toby Cracksman, in Newgate, to Bill Sykes].

I

prison

Dear Bill, this stone-jug at which flats dare to rail,
(From which till the next Central sittings I hail),
Is still the same snug, free-and-easy old hole,

mistresses

Where Macheath met his blowens, and Wild
[floor'd his bowl

friends

In a ward with one's pals, not locked up in a cell,

[Notes]

To an old hand like me it's a family hotel.

II

warders; bam-
boozle

In the dayrooms the cuffins we queers at our ease,

n'g't

And at Darkmans we run the rig just as we please,

meat and drink

There's your peck and your lush, hot and reg'lar
[each day.
All the same if you work, all the same if you
[play

greenhorn
tricks; talking
slang; obscenity

But the lark's when a goney up with us they shut
As ain't up to our lurks, our flash patter, and smut;

III

But soon in his eye nothing green would remain,
He knows what's o'clock when he comes out again.
And the next time he's quodded so downy   imprisoned
[and snug,
He may thank us for making him fly to the jug.   up to prison ways
But here comes a cuffin—who cuts short my tale,
It's agin rules is screevin' to pals out o' gaol.   writing

[The following postscript seems to have been
added when the Warder had passed.]

IV

For them coves in Guildhall, and that blessed
[Lord Mayor,
Prigs on their four bones should chop whiners   on knees should pray
[I swear:
That long over Newgit their Worships may rule,
As the high-toby, mob, crack and screeve model   highwayman; swell-mobsmen; burglars, forgers
[school;
For if Guv'ment wos here, not the Alderman's
[Bench,
Newgit soon 'ud be bad as 'the Pent,' or 'the   [Notes]
[Tench'.

THE LEARY MAN
[1857]

[From *The Vulgar Tongue*, by DUCANGE ANGLICUS].

I

Of ups and downs I've felt the shocks
Since days of bats and shuttlecocks,
And allcumpaine and Albert-rocks,
      When I the world began;
And for these games I often sigh
Both marmoncy and Spanish-fly,
And flying kites, too, in the sky,
      For which I've often ran.

II

But by what I've seen, and where I've been,
I've always found it so,
That if you wish to learn to live
      Too much you cannot know.
For you must now be wide-awake,
If a living you would make,
So I'll advise what course to take
      To be a Leary Man.

II

Go first to costermongery,
To every fakement get a-fly,   dodge; learn
And pick up all their slangery,
    But let this be your plan;
Put up with no Kieboshery,   nonsense
But look well after poshery,   money
And cut teetotal sloshery,   drink
    And get drunk when you can.

IV

And when you go to spree about,
Let it always be your pride
To have a white tile on your nob   hat; head
    And bull-dog by your side
Your fogle you must flashly tie   necktie
Each word must patter flashery,   talk slang
And hit cove's head to smashery,
    To be a Leary Man.

V

To Covent Garden or Billingsgate
You of a morn must not be late,
But your donkey drive at a slashing rate,
    And first be if you can.
From short pipe you must your bacca blow
And if your donkey will not go,
To lick him you must not be slow
    But well his hide must tan.

VI

The fakement conn'd by knowing rooks
Must be well known to you,
And if you come to fibbery,
      You must mug one or two.
[Notes] Then go to St Giles's rookery,
And live up some strange nookery,
Of no use domestic cookery,
      To be a Leary Man.

VII

Then go to pigeon fancery
And know each breed by quiz of eye,
Bald-heads from skin-'ems by their fly,
      Go wrong you never can.
All fighting coves too you must know
Ben Caunt as well as Bendigo,
And to each mill be sure to go,
      And be one of the van.

VIII

Things that are found before they're lost,
Be always first to find.
Restore dogs for a pound or two
      You'll do a thing that's kind,
And you must sport a blue billy,
handkerchief Or a yellow wipe tied loosily

Round your scrag for bloaks to see   neck; men
   That you're a Leary Man

IX

At knock-'em-downs and tiddlywink,
To be a sharp you must not shrink,
But be a brick and sport your chink   good   fellow;
                                         money
   To win must be your plan.
And set-toos and Cock-fighting
Are things you must take delight in,
And always try to be right in
   And every kidment scan.

X

And bullying and chaffing too,
To you should be well known,
Your nob be used to bruisery,   head; pugilism
   And hard as any stone.
Put the kiebosh on the dibbery,
Know a Joey from a tibbery,
And now and then have a black eye,
   To be a Leary Man.

XI

To fairs and races go must you,
And get in rows and fights a few,
And stopping out all night it's true
   Must often be your plan.

And as through the world you budgery,
Get well awake to fudgery,
And rub off every grudgery,
          And do the best you can.

XII

But mummery and slummery
You must keep in your mind,
For every day, mind what I say,
          Fresh fakements you will find.
But stick to this while you can crawl.
To stand 'till you're obliged to fall,
And when you're wide awake to all
          You'll be a Leary Man.

"A HUNDRED STRETCHES HENCE" [Notes]

[1859]

[From *The Vocabulum: or Rogues Lexicon*, by G. W. Matsell, New York].

I

Oh! where will be the culls of the bing	publicans
A hundred stretches hence?	years
The bene morts who sweetly sing,	pretty women
A hundred stretches hence?	
The autum-cacklers, autum-coves,	married women and men
The jolly blade who wildly roves ;	boon companion
And where the buffer, bruiser, blowen,	smuggler ; pugilist ; whore
And all the cops, and beaks so knowin,	police; magistrate
A hundred stretches hence ?	

II

And where the swag so bleakly pinched	plunder cleverly stolen
A hundred stretches hence?	
The thimbles, slangs, and danglers filched,	watches; chains; seals ; stolen
A hundred stretches hence?	
The chips, the fawneys, chatty-feeders,	money ; rings ; spoons
The bugs, the boungs, and well-filled readers;	breast-pins; purses pocket-book

receiver of stolen goods; brothel And where the fence, and snoozing ken,

thieves; drunk-ards With all the prigs and lushing men,

A hundred stretches hence?

III

Played out they lay, it will be said

A hundred stretches hence;

buried With shovels they were put to bed

A hundred stretches since!

taken to gaol had cheated a life sentence Some rubbed to wit had napped a winder,

hanged; drowned oneself And some were scragged and took a blinder,

get rid of the plunder Planted the swag and lost to sight,

We'll bid them one and all good-night,

A hundred stretches hence.

THE CHICKALEARY COVE   [Notes]

[*c.* 1864]

I

I'm a 'Chickaleary bloke' with my one, two, three,   Whitechapel swell
   Whitechapel was the village I was born in,
For to get me on the hop, or on my tibby drop,   get the better of me
   You must wake up very early in the morning.
I have a rorty gal, also a knowing pal,   flashly dressed; clever
   And merrily together we jog on,
I doesn't care a flatch, as long as I've a tach,   halfpenny; hat
   Some pannum for my chest, and a tog on.   eatables; coat
      I'm a Chickaleary bloke with my one, two,
                     [three,
      Whitechapel was the village I born in,
      For to get me on the hop, or on my
                    [tibby drop,
      You must wake up very early in the morning.

II

Now kool my downy kicksies—the style for me,   look; trousers flashly out
   Built on a plan werry naughty,
The stock around my squeeze a guiver colour see,   neck; flash

vest ; pockets   And the vestat with the bins so rorty,

teetotaller   My tailor serves you well, from a perger to a swell,

place   At Groves's you're safe to make a sure pitch,

money   For ready venom down, there ain't a shop in town.

beat   Can lick Groves in The Cut as well as Shoreditch.

I'm a Chickaleary bloke, etc.

III

Off to Paris I shall go, to show a thing or two

pickpockets   To the dipping blokes what hangs about the
[caffes,

[Notes]; watch;   How to do a cross-fam, for a super, or a slang,
chain

And to bustle them grand'armes I'd give the
[office :

Now my pals I'm going to slope, see you soon
[again, I hope,

My young woman is awaiting, so be quick;

salute ; shout   Now join in a chyike, the jolly we all like,

I'm off with a party to the Vic.

I'm a Chickaleary bloke, etc.

BLOOMING ÆSTHETIC   [Notes]

[1882]

[From *The Rag*, 30 Sept.].

He

I

A dealer-in-coke young man,
A wallop-his-moke young man,
A slosher-of-pals,
A spooning-with-gals,   making love
An ought-to-be-blowed young man.

II

A tell-a-good-whopper young man,   lie
A slogging-a-copper young man,   assaulting   the
                                                      police
A pay-on-the-nod,   take   unlimited
                                                      credit
An always-in-quod,   in prison
A sure-to-be-scragged young man.   hung

III

A Sunday-flash-togs young man,   clothes
A pocket-of-hogs young man,   silver
A save-all-his-rhino,   money
A cut-a-big-shine, oh,
Will soon-have-a-pub young man

She

I

A powder-and-paint young girl,
Not-quite-a-saint young girl,
drunk   An always-get-tight,
A stay-out-all-night,
ch ld   Have-a-kid-in-the-end young girl.

II

Make-a-bloke-a-choke young girl,
drunken bout   Love-a-gin-soak young girl,
On-the-kerb-come-a-cropper,
policeman   Run-in-by-a-copper,
" Fined-forty-bob "—young girl.

III

A tallow-faced-straight young girl,
A never-out-late young girl,
A Salvation-mummery,
Smoleless-and-glummery,
Kid-by-a-captain young girl.

'ARRY AT A POLITICAL PICNIC [Notes]

[By T Milliken in *Punch*, 11 Oct.]

DEAR CHARLIE.

I

'Ow are yer, my ribstone? Seems scrumtious to
    write the old name.
I 'ave quite lost the run of you lately. Bin playing   sight
    some dark little game?
I'm keeping mine hup as per usual, fust in the
    pick of the fun,
For wherever there's larks on the tappy there's
    'Arry as sure as a gun.

II

The latest new lay's Demonstrations. You've
    heard on 'em, Charlie, no doubt,
For they're at 'em all over the shop. I 'ave 'ad
    a rare bustle about.
All my Saturday arfs are devoted to Politics.
    Fancy, old chump,
Me doing the sawdusty reglar, and follering swells   nonsense
    on the stump!

But, bless yer, my bloater, it isn't all chin-music,
    votes, and ''Ear! 'ear!'
Or they wouldn't catch me on the ready, or nail
    me for ninepence. No fear!
Percessions I've got a bit tired of, hoof-padding
    and scrouging's dry rot,
But Political Picnics mean sugar to them as is
    fly to wot's wot.

talking appears in left margin beside the first couplet; *walking* appears beside the third.

IV

Went to one on 'em yesterday, Charlie; a reglar
    old up and down lark.
The Pallis free gratis, mixed up with a old country
    fair in a park,
And Rosherville Gardens chucked in, with a dash
    of the Bean Feast will do,
To give you some little idear of our day with
    Sir Jinks Bottleblue.

V

Make much of us, Charlie? Lor bless you, we
    might ha' bin blooming Chinese
A-doing the rounds at the 'Ealthrics. 'Twas
    regular go as you please.
Lawn-tennis, quoits, cricket, and dancing for them
    as must be on the shove,

But I preferred pecking and prowling, and spotting *eating*
    the mugs making love. *fools*

VI

Don't ketch me a-slinging my legs about arter
    a beast of a ball
At ninety degrees in the shade or so, Charlie,
    old chap, not at all.
Athletics 'aint 'ardly my form, and a cutaway
    coat and tight bags *trousers*
Are the species of togs for yours truly, and lick
    your loose 'flannels' to rags.

VII

So I let them as liked do a swelter; I sorntered
    about on the snap. *prowl*
Rum game this yer Politics, Charlie, seems arf
    talkee-talkee and trap.
Jest fancy old Bluebottle letting the 'multitood'
    pic-nic and lark,
And make Battersea Park of his pleasure-grounds,
    Bathelmy Fair of his park!

VIII

'To show his true love for the People!' sezs one
    vote-of-thanking tall-talker,
And wosn't it rude of a bloke as wos munching
    a bun to cry 'Walker!'? [Notes]

I'm Tory right down to my boots, at a price,
and I bellered ' 'Ear, 'ear!'

catch

But they don't cop yours truly with chaff none
the more, my dear Charlie, no fear!

IX

shook hands

Old Bottleblue tipped me his flipper, and 'oped
I'd ' refreshed,' and all that.

'Wy rather,' sez I, 'wot do you think?' at which
he stared into his 'at,

face

fool

And went a bit red in the gills. Must ha' thought
me a muggins, old man,

To ask sech a question of 'Arry—as though
grubbing short was his plan.

X

I went the rounds proper, I tell yer; 'twas like
the free run of a Bar,

And Politics wants lots o' wetting. Don't ketch
me perched up on a car,

Or 'olding a flag-pole no more. No, percessions,
dear boy, ain't my fad,

But Political Picnics with fireworks, and plenty
of swiz ain't 'arf bad.

XI

The palaver was sawdust and treacle. Old
Bottleblue buzzed for a bit,

And a sniffy young Wiscount in barnacles landed
    wot 'e thought a 'it;
Said old Gladstone wos like Simpson's weapon,
    a bit of a hass and all jor,
When a noisy young Rad in a widcawake wanted
    to give him what for! something to talk
                                about

XII

Yah! boo! Turn 'im hout!' sings yours truly,
    a-thinkin' the fun was at 'and,
But, bless yer! 'twas only a sputter. I can't say
    the meeting looked grand.
Five thousand they reckoned us, Charlie, but if
    so I guess the odd three
Were a-spooning about in the halley's, or lappin'
    up buns and Bohea.

XIII

The band and the 'opping wos prime though,
    and 'Arry in course wos all there.
I 'ad several turns with a snappy young party
    with stror coloured 'air.
Her name she hinformed me wos Polly, and wen
    in my 'appiest style,
I sez, ' Polly is nicer than Politics!' didn't she
    colour and smile?

XIV

We got back jest in time for the Fireworks, a
    proper flare-up, and no kid,

Which finished that day's Demonstration, an'
    must 'ave cost many a quid.
Wot fireworks and park-feeds do Demonstrate,
    Charlie, I'm blest if I see,
And I'm blowed if I care a brass button, so long
    as I get a cheap spree.

XV

The patter's all bow-wow, of course, but it goes
    with the buns and the beer.
If it pleases the Big-wigs to spout, wy it don't
    cost hus nothink to cheer.
Though they ain't got the 'ang of it, Charlie, the
    toffs ain't—no go and no spice!
Why, I'd back Barney Crump at our Singsong
    to lick 'em two times out o' twice!

XVI

Still I'm all for the Lords and their lot, Charlie.
    Rads are my 'orror, you know.
Change R into C and you've got 'em, and 'Arry
    'ates anythink low.
So if Demonstrations means skylarks, and lotion
    as much as you'll carry,
These ' busts of spontanyous opinion' may reckon
    all round upon 'Arry.

"RUM COVES THAT RELIEVE US" [Notes]
[1887]

[By HEINRICH BAUMANN in *Londonismen*].

I

Rum coves that relieve us   thieves
Of chinkers and pieces,   money
Is gin'rally lagged,   imprisoned
Or wuss luck gets scragg'd.   hung

II

Are smashers and divers   counterfeiters; pickpockets
And noble contrivers
Not sold to the beaks   magistrates
By the coppers an' sneaks?   police; informers

III

Yet moochin' arch-screevers,   prowling; begging letter writers
Concoctin' deceivers,
Chaps as reap like their own
What by tothers were sown;

IV

Piratical fakers   writers of " blood and thunder "
Of bosh by the acres,

These muck-worms of trash
Cut, oh, a great dash.

V

But, there, it don't matter
Since, to cut it still fatter,
By 'ook and by crook
Ve've got up this book.

VI

queer places   Tell ye 'ow? Vy in rum kens,
thieves' resorts   In flash cribs and slum dens,
I' the alleys and courts,
'Mong the doocedest sorts;

VII

When jawin' with Jillie
Or. Mag and 'er Billie,
Ve shoved down in black
talk   Their illigant clack.

VIII

So from hartful young dodgers,
men   From vaxy old codgers,
prostitutes   From the blowens ve got
Soon to know vot is vot.

IX

Now then there is yer sumptuous
Tuck-in of most scrumptious,
And dainty mag-pie!   speech
Will ye jes' come and try?

VILLON'S GOOD-NIGHT
[1887]

[By William Ernest Henley].

I

false clericos	You bible-sharps that thump on tubs,
beggar feigning sickness	You lurkers on the Abram-sham,
cadgers; loafing	You sponges miking round the pubs,
saucy girls; nonsense	You flymy titters fond of flam,
women; dress; game	You judes that clobber for the stramm,
[Notes]	You ponces good at talking tall,
rings; right hand	With fawneys on your dexter famm—
harlot [Notes]	A mot's good-night to one and all!

II

prostitutes;expose paps	Likewise you molls that flash your bubs
see; pay for	For swells to spot and stand you sam,
[Notes]	You bleeding bonnets, pugs, and subs,
Punch-and-Judy-man	You swatchel-coves that pitch and slam.
pattering tradesman	You magsmen bold that work the cram,
	You flats and joskins great and small,
wife	Gay grass-widows and lawful-jam—
	A mot's good-night to one and all!

III

For you, you coppers, narks, and dubs, *police; informers; warders*
Who pinched me when upon the snam, *arrested; stealing*
And gave me mumps and mulligrubs *"the blues"*
With skilly and swill that made me clam, *refuse food*
At you I merely lift my gam— *leg*
I drink your health against the wall! *urinate*
That is the sort of man I am,
A mot's good-night to one and all!

The Farewell.

Paste 'em, and larrup 'em, and lamm! *thrash them and make them stir*
Give Kennedy, and make 'em crawl!
I do not care one bloody damn,
A mot's good-night to one and all.

VILLON'S STRAIGHT TIP TO ALL CROSS COVES

[1887]

[By WILLIAM ERNEST HENLEY].

' *Tout aux tavernes et aux filles* '

I

[See Notes for translation]

Suppose you screeve, or go cheap-jack?
Or fake the broads? or fig a nag?
Or thimble-rig? or knap a yack?
Or pitch a snide? or smash a rag?
Suppose you duff? or nose and lag?
Or get the straight, and land your pot?
How do you melt the multy swag?
Booze and the blowens cop the lot.

II

Fiddle, or fence, or mace, or mack;
Or moskeneer, or flash the drag;
Dead-lurk a crib, or do a crack;
Pad with a slang, or chuck a mag;
Bonnet, or tout, or mump and gag;
Rattle the tats, or mark the spot

You cannot bank a single stag:
Booze and the blowens cop the lot.

III

Suppose you try a different tack,
And on the square you flash your flag?
At penny-a-lining make your whack,
Or with the mummers mug and gag?
For nix, for nix the dibbs you bag
At any graft, no matter what!
Your merry goblins soon stravag:
Booze and the blowens cop the lor.

The Moral.

It's up-the-spout and Charley-Wag
With wipes and tickers and what not!
Until the squeezer nips your scrag,
Booze and the blowens cop the lot.

[Notes]   # CULTURE IN THE SLUMS
[1887]

[By WILLIAM ERNEST HENLEY: "Inscribed to an intense poet"].

I. *Rondeau.*

I

"O crikey, Bill!" she ses to me, she ses.
"Look sharp," ses she, "with them there sossiges.
sausages   Yea! sharp with them there bags of mysteree!
friend   For lo!" she ses, "for lo! old pal," ses she,
very hungry   " I'm blooming peckish, neither more nor less."

II

Was it not prime—I leave you all to guess
girl   How prime! to have a jude in love's distress
fondling; softly   Come spooning round, and murmuring balm-
[ilee,
"O crikey, Bill!"

III

thus expressively For in such rorty wise doth Love express
[Notes]   His blooming views, and asks for your address,

And makes it right, and does the gay and free.
I kissed her—I did so! And her and me
Was pals. And if that ain't good business,
                    O crikey, Bill!

II. *Villanelle.*

I

Now ain't they utterly too-too   nice
(She ses, my Missus mine, ses she),
Them flymy little bits of Blue.   Notes] *i.e.* china

II

Joe, just you kool 'em—nice and skew   look at
Upon our old meogginee,
Now ain't they utterly too-too?

III

They're better than a pot'n a screw,
They're equal to a Sunday spree,
Them flymy little bits of Blue!

IV

Suppose I put 'em up the flue,   pawn
And booze the profits, Joe? Not me.   drink
Now ain't they utterly too-too?

V

I do the 'Igh Art fake, I do.
Joe, I'm consummate; and I *see*
Them flymy little bits of Blue.

VI

Which, Joe, is why I ses to you—
Æsthetic-like, and limp, and free—
Now ain't they utterly too-too,
Them flymy little bits of Blue?

III. *Ballade.*

I

I often does a quiet read
Botticelli(?)   At Booty Shelley's poetry;
I thinks that Swinburne at a screed
Is really almost too-too fly;
Wagner(?)   At Signor Vagna's harmony
I likes a merry little flutter;
I've had at Pater many a shy;
In fact, my form's the Bloomin' Utter.

II

My mark's a tidy little feed,
And 'Enery Irving's gallery,
To see old 'Amlick do a bleed,
And Ellen Terry on the die,
Or Franky's ghostes at hi-spy,
The Corsican   And parties carried on a shutter
Brothers(?)   Them vulgar Coupeaus is my eye!
In fact, my form's the Bloomin' Utter.

III

The Grosvenor's nuts—it is, indeed!
I goes for 'Olman 'Unt like pie.
It's equal to a friendly lead   [Notes]
To see B. Jones's judes go by.
Stanhope he makes me fit to cry,
Whistler he makes me melt like butter,
Strudwick he makes me flash my cly—   spend money
In fact, my form's the Bloomin' Utter.

Envoy.

I'm on for any Art that's 'Igh!
I talks as quite as I can splutter;
I keeps a Dado on the sly;
In fact, my form's the Blooming Utter!

"TOTTIE"

[1887]

[By "DAGONET" (G. R. SIMS) in *Referee*, 7 Nov.].

I

As she walked along the street

feet   With her little 'plates of meat,'
And the summer sunshine falling

hair   On her golden 'Barnet Fair,'
Bright as angels from the skies

eyes   Were her dark blue 'mutton pies.'

breast   In my 'East and West' Dan Cupid
Shot a shaft and left it there.

II

nose   She'd a Grecian 'I suppose,'

teeth   And of 'Hampstead Heath' two rows,

mouth   In her 'Sunny South' that glistened
Like two pretty strings of pearls;

knees   Down upon my 'bread and cheese'
Did I drop and murmur, 'Please

wife   Be my "storm and strife," dear Tottie,
O, you darlingest of girls!'

III

Then a bow-wow by her side,	dog
Who till then had stood and tried	
A 'Jenny Lee' to banish,	flee
Which was on his 'Jonah's whale,'	tail
Gave a hydrophobia bark,	
(She cried, 'What a Noah's Ark!')	lark
And right through my 'rank and riches'	breeches
Did my 'cribbage pegs' assail.	legs

IV

Ere her bull-dog I could stop	
She had called a 'ginger pop,'	slop = policeman
Who said, 'What the "Henry Meville"	devil
Do you think you're doing there?'	
And I heard as off I slunk,	
'Why, the fellow's "Jumbo's trunk!"'	drunk
And the 'Walter Joyce' was Tottie's	voice
With the golden 'Barnet Fair.'	hair

A PLANK BED BALLAD
[1888]

[By " DAGONET " (G. R. SIMS) in *Referee*, 12 Feb.].

I

Understand, if you please, I'm a travelling thief,
The gonophs all call me the gypsy;
By the rattler I ride when I've taken my brief,
And I sling on my back an old kipsey.

II

If I pipe a good chat, why, I touch for the wedge,
But I'm not a "particular" robber;
I smug any snowy I see on the hedge,
And I ain't above daisies and clobber.

III

One day I'd a spree with two finns in my brigh,
And a toy and a tackle—both red 'uns;
And a spark prop a pal (a good screwsman) and I
Had touched for in working two dead 'uns.

IV

I was taking a ducat to get back to town
(I had come by the rattler to Dover),

When I saw as a reeler was roasting me brown, *detective; closely scanning me*
And he rapped, " I shall just turn you over." *said; search you*

V

I guyed, but the reeler he gave me hot beef, *ran; tea; chased me*
And a scuff came about me and hollered;
I pulled out a chive, but I soon came to grief, *knife*
And with screws and a james I was collared. *burglars tools; caught*

VI

I was fullied, and then got three stretch for the job, *remanded; years*
And my trip—cuss the day as I seen her— *mistress*
She sold off my home to some pals in her mob, *friends; set*
For a couple of foont and ten deener. *£5 notes; shillings*

VII

Oh, donnys and omees, what gives me the spur, *girl; fellows*
Is, I'm told by a mug (he tells whoppers), *man [Notes]*
That I ought to have greased to have kept out *bribed*
                            [of stir
The dukes of the narks and the coppers. *hands; detectives; police*

THE RONDEAU OF THE KNOCK
[1890]

[By "DAGONET" (G. R. SIMS) in *Referee*, 20 Ap. p. 7].

I

gave in

He took the knock! No more with jaunty air
He'll have the "push" that made the punter stare;
£500
No more in monkeys now odds on he'll lay
And make the ever grumbling fielder gay.
opportunity
One plunger more has had his little flare
pay up
And then came to Monday when he couldn't
["square";
fellow
Stripped of his plunces a poor denuded J
He took the knock!
Where is he now? Ah! echo answers "where"?

Upon the turf he had his little day
ruined
And when, stone-broke, he could no longer
[pay
Leaving the ring to gnash its teeth and swear
He took the knock!

THE RHYME OF THE RUSHER   [Notes]

[1892]

[By Doss Chiderdoss in *Sporting Times*, 29 Oct.
In Appropriate Rhyming Slanguage.].

I

I was out one night on the strict teetote,   without drink
'Cause I couldn't afford a drain;
I was wearing a leaky I'm afloat,   coat
And it started to France and Spain.   rain
But a toff was mixed in a bull and cow,   swell; row
And I helped him to do a bunk;   get away
He had been on the I'm so tap, and now   rap
He was slightly elephant's trunk.   drunk

II

He offered to stand me a booze, so I   drink
Took him round to the "Mug's Retreat;"
And my round the houses I tried to dry   trousers
By the Anna Maria's heat.   fire
He stuck to the I'm so to drown his cares,
While I went for the far and near,   beer

stairs

Until the clock on the apples and pears

warning

Gave the office for us to clear.

III

Then round at the club we'd another bout,
And I fixed him at nap until

pockets

I had turned his skyrockets inside out,
And had managed my own to fill.

bounce

Of course, I had gone on the half-ounce trick,
And we quarrelled, and came to blows;
But I fired him out of the Rory quick,

nose

And he fell on his I suppose.

IV

And he laid there, weighing out prayers for me,

feet

Without hearing the plates of meat

policeman;arrest-
ed ; drunk and
disorderly

Of a slop, who pinched him for " d. and d."
And disturbing a peaceful beat.

eyes

And I smiled as I closed my two mince pies
In my insect promenade;

him ; advantage

For out of his nibs I had taken a rise,
And his stay on the spot was barred.

V

hair

Next morning I brushed up my Barnet Fair,
And got myself up pretty smart;
Then I sallied forth with a careless air,

heart

And contented raspberry tart.

At the first big pub I resolved, if pos.,   possible
    That I'd sample my lucky star;
So I passed a flimsy on to the boss   banknote
    Who served drinks at the there you are.   bar

VI

He looked at the note, and the air began
    With his language to pen and ink;   stink
For the mug I'd fleeced had been his head man,   fellow; cheated
    And had done him for lots of chink.   robbed; money
I'm blessed if my luck doesn't hum and ha,
    For I argued the point with skill;
But the once a week made me go ta-ta   beak
    For a month on the can't keep still.   everlasting
                                             wheel = mill

WOT CHER!

or, Knocked 'em in the Old Kent Rd.

[1892]

[By Albert Chevalier].

I

well-dressed man Last week down our alley come a toff,

man Nice old geezer with a nasty cough,

hat Sees my Missus, takes 'is topper off
    In a very gentlemanly way!
"Ma'am," says he, "I 'ave some news to tell,
Your rich Uncle Tom of Camberwell,

died; mistake Popped off recent, which it ain't a sell,
    Leaving you 'is little Donkey Shay.
    "Wot cher!" all the neighbours cried,
    " Who're yer goin' to meet, Bill?
    Have yer bought the street, Bill?"
    Laugh! I thought I should 'ave died,

made them stare Knock'd 'em in the Old Kent Road!

II

donkey Some says nasty things about the moke,

fellow One cove thinks 'is leg is really broke,
That's 'is envy, cos we're carriage folk,

Like the toffs as rides in Rotten Row!
Straight! it woke the alley up a bit,   no mistake
Thought our lodger would 'ave 'ad a fit,
When my missus, who's a real wit,
　　Says, "I 'ates a Bus, because it's low!"
　　　　" Wot cher !" &c.

III

When we starts the blessed donkey stops,
He won't move, so out I quickly 'ops,
Pals start whackin' him, when down he drops,
　　Someone says he wasn't made to go.
Lor it might 'ave been a four-in-'and,
My Old Dutch knows 'ow to do the grand,   wife; make a show
First she bows, and then she waves 'er 'and,
　　Calling out we're goin' for a blow !
　　　　"Wot cher !" &c.

IV

Ev'ry evenin' on the stroke of five,
Me and Missus takes a little drive,
You'd say, " Wonderful they're still alive,"
　　If you saw that little donkey go.
I soon showed him that 'e 'd have to do
Just whatever he was wanted to,
Still I shan't forget that rowdy crew,
　　'Ollerin' " Woa! steady! Neddy Woa!
　　　　"Wot cher !" &c.

[Notes]

OUR LITTLE NIPPER
[1893]

[By Albert Chevalier].

I

I'm just about the proudest man that walks,
child I've got a little nipper, when 'e talks
shillings; pound I'll lay yer forty shiners to a quid
You'll take 'im for the father, me the kid.
Now as I never yet was blessed wi' wealf,
I've 'ad to bring that youngster up myself,
And though 'is education 'as been free,
infamation 'E's allus 'ad the best of tips from me.
            And 'e's a little champion,
[Notes]   Do me proud well 'e's a knock out,
    Takes after me and ain't a bit too tall.
    'E calls 'is mother "Sally,"
    And 'is father "good old pally,"
    And 'e only stands about so 'igh, that's all!

II

[Notes] 'E gits me on at skittles and 'e flukes,
hands And when 'e wants to 'e can use 'is "dooks,"
You see 'im put 'em up, well there, it's great,

'E takes a bit of lickin at 'is weight;
'E'll stick up like a Briton for 'is pals,
An' ain't 'e just a terror with the gals;
I loves to see 'im cuttin' of a dash,
A walkin' down our alley on the mash.　　　courting
　　　There, 'e's a little champion,
　　　Do me proud well 'e's a knock out,
　　　I've knowed 'im take a girl on six foot tall;
　　　'E'll git 'imself up dossy,　　　dressy
　　　Say I'm goin' out wi' Flossie,
　　　An' 'e only stands about so 'igh, that's all.

III

I used to do a gin crawl e'vry night,　　　round of ginshops
An' very, very often come 'ome tight,　　　drunk
But now of all sich 'abits I've got rid,
I allus wants to git 'ome to the kid.
In teachin' 'im I takes a regular pride,
Not books, of course, for them 'e can't abide,
But artful little ikey little ways,　　　funny
As makes the people sit up where we stays.　　　stare

(*Spoken*)—Only last Sunday me an' the missus
took 'im out for a walk—I should say 'e took
us out. As we was a comin' 'ome I says to the
old gal "Let's pop into the 'Broker's Arms' and
'ave a drop o' beer?" She didn't raise no
objection so in we goes, followed by 'is nibs—I'd
forgotten all about 'im—I goes to the bar and

calls for two pots of four 'alf; suddenly I feels
'im a tuggin' at my coat, "Wot's up?" sez I;
"Wot did yer call for?" sez 'e; "Two pots of
four 'alf," sez I; "Oh," sez 'e, "ain't mother
goin' to 'ave none?"

Well, 'e's a little champion,
Do me proud well 'e's a knock out,
"Drink up," sez 'e, "Three pots, miss, it's
I sez "Now Jacky, Jacky;"   [my call."
'E sez, "And a screw of baccy,"
And 'e only stands about so 'igh, that's all.

THE COSTER'S SERENADE   [Notes]

[1894]

[By ALBERT CHEVALIER].

I

You ain't forgotten yet that night in May,
Down at the Welsh 'Arp, which is 'Endon way,
You fancied winkles and a pot of tea,
" Four 'alf" I murmured's " good enough for me."
" Give me a word of 'ope that I may win"—
You prods me gently with the winkle pin—
We was as 'appy as could be that day
Down at the Welsh 'Arp, which is 'Endon way.

   Oh, 'Arriet I'm waiting, waiting for you my dear,
   Oh, 'Arriet I'm waiting, waiting alone out here ;
     When that moon shall cease to shine,
     False will be this 'eart of mine,
   I'm bound to go on lovin' yer my dear; d'ye 'ear?

II

You ain't forgotten 'ow we drove that day
Down to the Welsh 'Arp, in my donkey shay ;

shout

Folks with a "chy-ike" shouted, "Ain't they smart?"
You looked a queen, me every inch a Bart.
Seemed that the moke was saying "Do me proud;"

finest; trap

Mine is the nobbiest turn-out in the crowd;

[Notes]; swell

Me in my "pearlies" felt a toff that day,
Down at the Welsh 'Arp, which is Endon way.
  Oh, 'Arriet, &c.

III

Eight months ago and things is still the same,
You're known about 'ere by your maiden name,

chaffed

I'm getting chivied by my pals 'cos why?
Nightly I warbles 'ere for your reply.
Summer 'as gone, and it's a freezin' now,
Still love's a burnin' in my 'eart, I vow;
Just as it did that 'appy night in May
Down at the Welsh 'Arp, which is Endon way.
  Oh, 'Arriet, &c.

NOTES

Rhymes of the Canting Crew*

THESE lines are of little interest apart from the fact of being the earliest known example of the Canting speech or Pedlar's French in English literature. Sorry in point or meaning, they are sorrier still as verse. Yet, antedating, by half a century or more, the examples cited by Awdeley and Harman, they possess a certain value they carry us back almost to the beginnings of Cant, at all events to the time when the secret language of rogues and vagabonds first began to assume a concrete form.

Usually ascribed to Thomas Dekker (who "conveyed" them bodily, and with errors, to *Lanthorne and Candlelight*, published in 1609) this jingle of popular Canting phrases, strung together almost at hap-hazard, is the production of Robert Copland (1508—1547), the author of *The Hye Way to the Spyttel House*, a pamphlet printed after 1535, and of which only two or three copies are now known. Copland was a printer-author; in the former capacity a pupil of Caxton in the office of Wynkyn de Worde.

The plan of *The Hye Way* is simplicity itself. Copland, taking refuge near St. Bartholomew's Hospital during a passing shower, engages the porter in conversation concerning the "losels, mighty beggars and vagabonds, the michers, hedge-creepers, fylloks and luskes" that "ask lodging for Our Lord's sake". Thereupon is drawn a vivid and vigorous picture of the seamy side of the social life of the times. All grades of "vagrom men," with their frauds and shifts, are passed in review, and when Copland asks about their "bousy" speech, the porter entertains him with these lines.

Lines 2 and 4. *Bousy* = drunken, sottish, dissipated. So Skelton in *Elynoor Rommin* (Harl. MSS. ed. Park, 1. 416), 'Her face all *bowsie*'. *Booze* = to drink heavily, is still colloquial; and, = to drink, was in use as early as A.D. 1300. Line 4. *Cove* (or *Cofe*) = a man, an individual. *Maimed nace* (*nase* or *nazy*) = helplessly drunk; Lat. *nausea* = sickness; *cf.* line 9, '*nace gere*'. Line 5. *Teare* (*toure* or *towre*) = to look, to see. *Patrying cove* (*patrico, patricove,* or *pattercove*) = a strolling priest; *cf.* Awdeley, *Frat. of Vacabondes* (1560), p. 6.:— "A Patriarke Co. doth make marriages, and that is untill death depart the married folke, which is after this sort: When they come to a dead Horse or any dead Catell, then they shake hands and so depart, euery one of them a seuerall way." The form *patrying cove* seems to suggest a derivation from 'pattering' or 'muttering'—the Pater-noster, up to the time of the Reformation, was recited by the priest in a low voice as far as 'and lead us not into temptation' when the choir joined in. *Darkman cace* (or *case*) = a sleeping apartment or place—ward, barn, or inn: *darkmans* = night + Lat. *casa* = house etc.: '*mans*' is a common canting affix = a thing or place: *e.g. lightmans* = day; *ruffmans* = a wood or bush; *greenmans* = the fields; *Chepemans* = Cheapside market etc. Line **6.** *docked the dell* = deflowered the girl: *dell* = virgin; see Harman, *Caveat* (1575), p. 75:—'A dell is a yonge wenche, able for generation, and not yet knowen or broken by the upright man'. *Coper meke* (or *make*) = a half-penny. Line **7.** *His watch* = he: *my watch* = I, or me: *cf.* 'his nabs' and 'my nabs' in modern slang. *Feng* (A. S.) = to get, to steal, to snatch. *Prounces nob-chete* = prince's hat or cap: *cheat* (A. S.) = thing, and mainly used as an affix: thus, *belly-chete* = an apron; *cackling-chete* = a fowl; *crash-ing-chetes* = the teeth; *nubbing-chete* = the gallows, and so forth. Line **8.** *Cyarum, by Salmon*—the meaning of *cyarum* is unknown: *by Salmon* (or *Solomon*) = a beggar's oath, *i.e.*, by the altar or mass. *Pek my jere* = eat excrement: *cf.* 'turd in your mouth'. Line **9.** *gan* = mouth. *My watch*, see *ante*, line **7.** *Nace gere* = nauseous stuff: *cf. ante*, line **4:** *gere* = generic for thing, stuff, or material. Line **10.** *bene bouse* = strong drink or wine.

The Beggar's Curse

Thomas Dekker, one of the best known of the Elizabethan pamphleteers and dramatists, was born in London about 1570, and began his literary career in 1597-8 when an entry referring to a loan-advance occurs in Henslowe's *Diary*. A month later forty shillings were advanced from the same source to have him discharged from the Counter, a debtor's prison. Dekker was a most voluminous writer, and not always over-particular whence he got, or how he used, the material for his tracts and plays. *The Belman of London Bringing to Light the Most Notorious Villanies that are now practised in the Kingdome* (1608) of which three editions were published in one year, consists mainly of pilferings from Harman's *Caveat for Common Cursetors* first published in 1566-7. He did not escape conviction, however, for Samuel Rowlands showed him up in *Martin Mark-All*. Yet another instance of wholesale "conveyance" is mentioned in the Note to "Cant-ing Rhymes" (*ante*). In spite of this shortcoming, however, and a certain recklessness of workman-ship, the scholar of to-day owes Dekker a world of thanks: his information concerning the social life of his time is such as can be obtained nowhere else, and it is, therefore, now of sterling value.

Lanthorne and Candlelight is the second part of *The Belman of London*. Published also in 1608, it ran to two editions in 1609, a fourth appearing in 1612 under the title of *O per se O, or a new Cryer of Lanthorne and Candlelight, Being an Addition or Lengthening of the Belman's Second Night Walke.* Eight or nine editions of this second part appeared between 1608 and 1648 all differing more or less from each other, another variation occurring when in 1637 Dekker republished *Lanthorne and Candlelight* under the title of *English Villanies*, shortly after which he is supposed to have died.

"Towre Out Ben Morts"

Samuel Rowlands, a voluminous writer *circa* 1570—1628, though little known now, nevertheless kept the publishers busy for thirty years, his works selling readily for another half century. Not the least valuable of his numerous productions from a social and antiquarian point of view is *Martin Mark-All, Beadle of Bridewell; his Defence and Answere to the Belman of London* (see both Notes *ante*).

Martin Markall delivers himself of a vivid and "originall" account of "the Regiment of Rogues, when they first began to take head, and how they have succeeded one the other successively unto the sixth and twentieth year of King Henry the Eighth, gathered out of the Chronicle of Crackropes" etc. He then criticizes somewhat severely the errors and omissions in Dekker's Canting glossary, adding considerably to it, and finally joins issue with the Belman in an attempt to give "song for song". Dekker's "Canting Rhymes" (plagiarised from Copland) and "The Beggar's Curse" thus apparently gave birth to the present verses and to those entitled "The Maunder's Wooing" that follow.

Stanza I, line 1. *Ben* = Lat. *bene* = good. *Mort* = a woman, chaste or not. Line 3. *Rome-cove* = "a great rogue" (B. E., *Dict. Cant. Crew*, 1690), *i.e.*, an organizer, or the actual perpetrator of a robbery: *quire-cove* = a subordinate thief—the money had passed from the actual thief to his confederate. *Rom* (or *rum*) and *quier* (or *queer*) enter largely into combination, thus —*rom* = gallant, fine, clever, excellent, strong; *rom-bouse* = wine or strong drink; *rum-bite* = a clever trick or fraud; *rum-blowen* = a handsome mistress; *rum-bung* = full purse; *rum-diver* = a clever pickpocket; *rum-padder* = a well-mounted highwayman, etc.: also *queere* = base, roguish; *queer-bung* = an empty purse; *queer-cole* = bad money; *queer-diver* = a bungling pickpocket; *queer-ken* = a prison; *queer-mort* = a foundered whore, and so forth. *Budge* = a general verb of action, usually stealthy action: thus, *budge a beak* = to give the constable the slip, or to bilk a policeman; *to budge out* (or *off*) = to sneak off; *to budge an alarm* = to give warning.

The Maunder's Wooing

See previous Note.

Stanza II, line **2**. *Autem mort* = a wife; thus Harman, *Caveat* (1575):—"These Autem Mortes be maried wemen, as there be but a fewe. For Autem in their Language is a Churche; so she is a wyfe maried at the Church, and they be as chaste as a Cowe I have, that goeth to Bull every moone, with what Bull she careth not." Line **5**. *wap* = to lie carnally with.

Stanza IV, line **5**. *Whittington* = Newgate, from the famous Lord Mayor of London who left a bequest to rebuild the gaol. After standing for 230 years Whittington's building was demolished in 1666.

Stanza V, line **2**. *Crackmans* = hedges or bushes. *Tip lowr with thy prat* = (literally) get money with thy buttocks, *i.e.* ·by prostitution.

Stanza VI, line **1**. *Clapperdogen* = (B. E. *Dict. Cant. Crew*, 1690) "a beggar born and bred"; also Harman, *Caveat*, etc. p. 44:—"these go with patched clokes, and have their morts with them, which they call wives."

"A Gage of ben Rom-bouse"

Thomas Middleton, another of the galaxy of Elizabethan writers contributing so many sidelights on Shakspeare's life and times, is supposed to have been of gentle birth. He entered Gray's Inn about 1593 and was associated with Dekker in the production of *The Roaring Girl*, probably having the larger share in the composition. Authorities concur in tracing Dekker's hand in the canting scenes, but less certainly elsewhere. The original of Moll Cut-purse was a Mary Frith (1584—1659), the daughter of a shoemaker in the Barbican. Though carefully brought up she was particularly restive under discipline, and finally became launched as a "bully, pickpurse, fortune-teller, receiver and forger" in all of which capacities she achieved considerable notoriety. As the heroine of *The Roaring Girl* Moll is presented in a much more favorable light than the facts warrant.

Line 11. *And couch till a palliard docked my dell* = (literally) 'And lie quiet while a beggar deflowered my girl', but here probably = while a beggar fornicates with my mistress.

"Bing Out, Bien Morts"

[*See* Note to "The Beggar's Curse"]. Dekker introducing these verses affirms "it is a canting song not ... composed as those of the Belman's were, out of his owne braine, but by the Canter's themselves, and sung at their meetings", in which, all things considered, Dekker is probably protesting overmuch.

Stanza V, line 3. *And wapping dell that niggles well* = a harlot or mistress who "spreads" acceptably.

Stanza IX, line 2. *Bing out of the Rom-vile;*

i.e. to Tyburn, then the place of execution : *Rom-vile* = London.

The Song of the Beggar

The Description of Love is an exceedingly scarce little "garland" which first appeared in 1620; but of that edition no copies are known to exist. Of the sixth edition, from which this example is taken, one copy is in the British Museum and another in the library collected by Henry Huth Esq. A somewhat similar ballad occurs in the Roxburgh Collection I, 42 (the chorus being almost identical), under the title of " The Cunning Northern Beggar". The complete title is *A Description of Love. With certain Epigrams, Elegies, and Sonnets. And also Mast. Iohnson's Answere to Mast. Withers. With the Crie of Ludgate, and the Song of the Begger. The sixth Edition. London, Printed by M. F. for* FRANCIS COULES *at the Upper end of the Old-Baily neere Newgate,* 1629.

Stanza II, line 1. *If a Bung be got by the Hie-law,* *i.e.* by Highway robbery.

The Maunder's Initiation

John Fletcher (1579—1625), dramatist, a younger son of Dr. Richard Fletcher afterwards bishop of London, by his first wife Elizabeth, was born in December 1579 at Rye in Sussex, where his father was then officiating as minister. A 'John Fletcher of London' was admitted 15 Oct. 1591 a pensioner of Bene't (Corpus) College, Cambridge, of which college Dr. Fletcher had been president. Dyce assumes that this John Fletcher, who became one of the bible-clerks in 1593, was the dramatist. Bishop Fletcher died, in needy circumstances, 15 June 1596, and by his will, dated 26 Oct. 1593, left his books to be divided between his sons Nathaniel and John.

The Beggar's Bush was performed at Court at Christmas 1622, and was popular long after the Restoration.

Fletcher was buried on 29 Aug. 1625 at St. Saviour's, Southwark. 'In the great plague, 1625,' says Aubrey (*Letters written by Eminent Persons*, vol. ii. pt. i. p. 352), 'a knight of Norfolk or Suffolk invited him into the countrey. He stayed but to make himselfe a suite of cloathes, and while it was makeing fell sick of the plague and died.'

The High Pad's Boast

See Note to "The Maunder's, Initiation", *ante*.

The Merry Beggars

Little is known of the birth or extraction of Richard Brome, and whether he died in 1652 or 1653 is uncertain. For a time he acted as servant to Ben Jonson. *The Jovial Crew* was produced in 1641 at The Cock-pit, a theatre which stood on the site of Pitt Place running out of Drury Lane into Gt. Wild St.

Stanza I, line **5**. *Go-well and Com-well* = outgoing and incoming.

A Mort's Drinking. Song

See Note to "The Merry Beggars," *ante.*

"A Beggar I'll Be"

This ballad is from the Bagford Collection which, formed by John Bagford (1651—1716), passed successively through the hands of James West (president of the Royal Society), Major Pearson, the Duke of Roxburghe and Mr. B. H. Bright, until in 1845 it and the more extensive Roxburghe Collection became the property of the nation.

Stanza II, line 1. *Maunder* = beggar. Line 2. *filer* = pickpocket; *filcher* = thief. Line 3. *canter* = a tramping beggar or rogue. Line 4. *lifter* = a shop-thief.

Stanza IV, line 8. *Compter* (or *Counter*), *King's Bench, nor the Fleet*, all prisons for debtors.

Stanza V, line 6. *jumble* = to copulate.

Stanza VIII, line 5. *With Shinkin-ap-Morgan, with Blue-cap, or Teague* = With a Welshman, Scotchman, or Irishman—generic: as now are Taffy, Sandy, and Pat.

A Budg and Snudg Song

Chappell in *Popular English Music of the Olden Time* says that this song appears in *The Canting Academy* (2nd ed. 1674) but the writer has been unable to find a copy of the book in question. The song was very popular, and many versions (all varying) are extant. The two given have been carefully collated. The portions in brackets [ ],—for example stanza II, line 6, stanza III, lines 1—7, stanza IV, lines 5—8 etc.—only appear

in the *New Canting Dict.* (1725). It was sung
to the tune now known as *There was a jolly miller
once lived on the river Dee.*

Title. *Budge =* "one that slips into a house
in the dark, and taketh cloaks, coats, or what
comes next to hand, marching off with them"
(B. E., *Dict. Cant. Crew*, 1690). *Snudge =* "one
that lurks under a bed, to watch an opportunity
to rob the house"—(B. E., *Dict. Cant. Crew*,
1690).

Stanza I, line 7. *Whitt =* Newgate (*see* Note
p. 204).

Stanza V, line 3. *Jack Ketch,* the public hangman 1663—1686.

The Maunder's Praise of His
Strowling Mort

The Triumph of Wit by J. Shirley is a curious
piece of bookmaking—scissors and paste in
the main—which ran through many editions.
Divided into three parts, the first two are chiefly
concerned with "the whole art and mystery of
love in all its nicest intrigues", "choice letters
with their answers" and such like matters. Part
III contains "the mystery and art of Canting,
with the original and present management thereof,
and the ends to which it serves, and is employed:
Illustrated with poems, songs and various intrigues
in the Canting language with the explanation,
etc." The songs were afterwards included in *The
New Canting Dict.* (1725), and later on in *Bacchus
and Venus* (1731).

Title. *Strowling Mort =* a beggar's trull:—"pretending to be widows, sometimes travel the coun-
tries . . . are light-fingered, subtle, hypocritical,

14

cruel, and often dangerous to meet, especially when the ruffler is with them " (B. E., *Dict. Cant. Crew*, 1690).

Stanza I, line 1. *Doxy*—"These Doxes be broken and spoyled of their maydenhead by the upright men, and then they have their name of Doxes, and not afore. And afterwards she is commen and indifferent for any that wyll use her".—Harman, *Caveat*, p. 73. Line **3**. *prats* = buttocks or thighs. Line 4. *wap* = to copulate (also stanza IV, line 1).

Stanza II, line 4. *clip and kiss* = to copulate.

The Rum-Mort's Praise of Her Faithless Maunder

Obviously a companion song to the previous example: *See* Note *ante*. *Rum-Mort* = a beggar or gypsy queen.

Stanza I, line 1. *Kinching-cove* = (literally) a child or young lad: here as an endearment. Line 4. *Clapperdogeon* = "The Paillard or Clapperdogeons, are those that have been brought up to beg from their infancy, and frequently counterfeit lameness, making their legs, arms, and hands appear to be sore"—*Triumph of Wit*, p. 185.

Stanza II, line 1. *Dimber-damber* = a chief man in the Canting Crew, or the head of a gang. Line 2. *Palliard* (*See* note Stanza I). Line **3**. *jockum* = *penis*. Line 4. *glimmer* = fire: here, a pox or clap.

Stanza V, line 1. *crank* (or *counterfeit-crank*)— "These that do counterfet the cranke be yong knaves and yonge harlots that deeply dissemble the falling sickness".—(Harman, *Caveat*, 1814, p. 33). Line 1. *dommerar* = a beggar feigning deaf and dumb. Line **2.** *rum-maunder* = to feign madness. Line **3.** *Abram-cove* = a beggar pretending madness to cover theft. Line **4.** *Gybes well jerk'd* = pass or license cleverly forged.

The Black Procession

See Note as to J. Shirley on page 209.

Frisky Moll's Song

John Harper (*d.* 1742), actor, originally performed at Bartholomew and Southwark fairs. On 27 Oct. 1721 his name appears as Sir Epicure Mammon in the *Alchemist* at Drury Lane. Here he remained for eleven years, taking the parts of booby squires, fox-hunters, etc., proving himself what Victor calls 'a jolly facetious low comedian'. His good voice was serviceable in ballad opera and farce. On account of his 'natural timidity', according to Davies, he was selected by Highmore, the patentee, in order to test the status of an actor, to be the victim of legal proceedings taken under the Vagrant Act, 12 Queen Anne, and on 12 Nov. 1733 he was committed to Bridewell as a vagabond. On 20 Nov. he came before the chief justice of the Kings Bench. It was pleaded on his behalf that he paid his debts, was well esteemed by persons of condition, was a freeholder in Surrey, and a householder in Westminster. He was discharged amid acclamations on his own recognisance.

The Canter's Serenade

The New Canting Dictionary (1725) is, in the main, a reprint of *The Dictionary of the Canting*

Crew (*c.* 1696) compiled by B. E. The chief difference is that the former contains a collection of Canting Songs, most of which are included in the present collection.

Stanza I, line 3. *palliards—see* Note, p. 210, ten lines from bottom.

"Retoure my dear dell"

See Note to "The Canter's Serenade." This song appears to be a variation of a much older one, generally ascribed to Chas II, entitled *I pass all my hours in a shady old grove.*

The Vain Dreamer

See Note to "The Canter's Serenade."

"When my Dimber Dell I Courted"

See Note to "The Canter's Serenade." The first two stanzas appear in a somewhat different form as "a new song" to the time of *Beauty's Ruin* in *The Triumph of Wit* (1707), of which the first stanza is as follows:—

When Dorinda first I courted,
    She had charms and beauty too;
Conquering pleasures when she sported,
    The transport it was ever new:
But wastful time do's now deceive her,
    Which her glories did uphold;
All her arts can ne'er relieve her,
    Poor Dorinda is grown old.

Stanza I, line 4. *Wap* = the act of kind. *Dimber dell* = pretty wench—"A dell is a yonge wenche, able for generation, and not yet knowen or broken by the upright man . . . when they have beene lyen with all by the upright man then they be Doxes, and no Dells."—(HARMAN).

Stanza III, line 3. *Upright-men*—"the second rank of the Canting tribes, having sole right to the first night's lodging with the Dells."—(B. E., *Dict. Cant. Crew*, 1696).

The Oath of the Canting Crew

Bamfylde Moore Carew, the King of the Gypsies, born in 1693, was the son of the Rector of Bickley, near Tiverton. It is related that to avoid punishment for a boyish freak he, with some companions, ran away and joined the gypsies. After a year and a half Carew returned for a time, but soon rejoined his old friends. His career was a long series of swindling and imposture, very ingeniously carried out, occasionally deceiving people who should have known him well. His restless nature then drove him to embark for Newfoundland, where he stopped but a short time, and on his return he pretended to be the mate of a vessel, and eloped with the daughter of a respectable apothecary of Newcastle on Tyne, whom he afterwards married. He continued his course of vagabond roguery for some time, and when Clause Patch, a king, or chief of the gypsies, died, Carew was elected his successor. He was convicted of being an idle vagrant, and sentenced to be transported to Maryland. On his arrival he attempted to escape, was captured, and made to wear a heavy iron collar, escaped again, and fell into the hands of some friendly Indians,

who relieved him of his collar. He took an early
opportunity of leaving his new friends, and got
into Pennsylvania. Here he pretended to be a
Quaker, and as such made his way to Philadel-
phia, thence to New York, and afterwards to
New London, where he embarked for England.
He escaped impressment on board a man-of-war
by pricking his hands and face, and rubbing in
bay salt and gunpowder, so as to simulate small-
pox. After his landing he continued his impostures,
found out his wife and daughter, and seems to
have wandered into Scotland about 1745, and is
said to have accompanied the Pretender to Car-
lisle and Derby. The record of his life from this
time is but a series of frauds and deceptions, and
but little is absolutely known of his career, except
that a relative, Sir Thomas Carew of Hackern,
offered to provide for him if he would give up
his wandering life. This he refused to do, but
it is believed that he eventually did so after he
had gained some prizes in the lottery. The date
of his death is uncertain. It is generally given,
but on no authority, as being in 1770 but 'I. P.',
writing from Tiverton, in *Notes and Queries*, 2nd
series, vol. IV, p. 522, says that he died in 1758.
The story of his life in detail is found in the well-
known, and certainly much-printed, *Life and Adventures of Bamfylde Moore Carew*, the earliest edition
of which (1745) describes him on the title-page as
"the Noted Devonshire Stroller and Dogstealer".
This book professes to have been "noted by
himself during his passage to America", but though
no doubt the facts were supplied by Carew himself, the actual authorship is uncertain, though
the balance of probability lies with Robert Goadby,
a printer and compiler of Sherborne Dorsetshire,
who printed an edition in 1749. A correspondent
of *Notes and Queries*, however, states that Mrs.

Goadby wrote it from Carew's dictation. [*N. and Q.* 2 S iii. 4; iv. 330, 440, 522].

Line 1. *Crank Cuffin* = *Queer Cove* = a rogue. Line 9. *Stop-hole Abbey*, "the nick-name of the chief rendezvous of the Canting Crew".—(B. E., *Dict. Cant. Crew*, 1696). Line 17. *Abram* = formerly a mendicant lunatic of Bethlehem Hospital who on certain days was allowed to go out begging: hence a beggar feigning madness. *Ruffler crack* = an expert rogue. Line 18. *Hooker* = "peryllous and most wicked Knaves ... for, as they walke a day times, from house to house, to demaund Charite ... well noting what they see ... that will they be sure to have ... for they customably carry with them a staffe of V. of VI. foote long, in which within one ynch of the tope thereof, ys a lytle hole bored through, in which hole they putte an yron hoke, and with the same they wyll pluck unto them quickly anything that they may reche therewith."—(Harman, *Caveat*, 1869, p. 35, 36). Line 19. *Frater* = "such as beg with a sham-patent or brief for Spitals, Prisons, Fires, etc."—(B. E.). Line 20. *Irish toyle* = a beggar-thief, working under pretence of peddling pins, lace, and such-like wares. Line 21. *Dimber-damber* = the chief of a gang: also an expert thief. *Angler* = hooker (see *ante*). Line 23. *swigman* = a beggar peddling haberdashery to cover theft and roguery. *Clapperdogeon* = a beggar born and bred, *see* note p. 210, tenth line from bottom. Line 24. *Curtal*—"a curtall is much like to the upright man (that is, one in authority, who may "call to account", "command a share", chastise those under him, and "force any of their women to serve his turn"), but hys authority is not fully so great. He useth commonly to go with a short cloke, like to grey Friers, and his woman with

him in like livery, which he calleth his Altham
if she be hys wyfe, and if she be his harlot, she is
called hys Doxy."—(HARMAN). Line 25. *Whip-
jack* = a rogue begging with a counterfeit license.
Palliard = a beggar born and bred. *Patrico* =
a hedge-priest. Line 26. *Jarkman* = "he that
can write and reade, and sometime speake latin.
He useth to make counterfaite licenses which
they call gybes, and sets to scales, in their language called Jarkes."—(HARMAN). Line 27. *Dommerar* = a rogue pretending deaf and dumb.
Romany = a gipsy. Line 28. *The family* = the
fraternity of vagabonds.

"Come All You Buffers Gay"

In the Roxburghe Collection (ii. 504) is a ballad
upon which the present song is clearly based.
It is called *The West Country Nymph*, or *the
little maid of Bristol* to the time of *Young Jemmy*
(*i.e.* the Duke of Monmouth, Charles II's natural
son). The first stanza runs—

> Come all you maidens fair,
>   And listen to my ditty,
> In Bristol city fair
>   There liv'd a damsel pretty.

The Potato Man

Stanza II, line 2. *Cly* = properly pocket, but
here is obviously meant the contents.

Stanza IV, line 1. *Blue bird's-eye* = a blue and
silk handkerchief with white spots.

A Slang Pastoral

Of R. Tomlinson nothing is known. The
Dr. Byrom whose poem is here parodied is per-

haps best remembered as the author of a once famous system of shorthand. He was born in 1691, went to the Merchant Taylor's School, and at the age of 16 was admitted a pensioner of Trinity College Cambridge. It was here that he wrote *My time, O ye muses*. He died in 1763, and his poems, no inconsiderable collection, were published in 1773.

"Ye Scamps, Ye Pads, Ye Divers"

Stanza I, line 1. *The lay* = a pursuit, a scheme: here = thievery and roguery in general.

Stanza IV, line 4. *Like Blackamore Othello &c.*— the reference is to *Othello*, v. 2. "Yet she must die, else she'll betray more men. Put out the light, and then—put out the light."

The Sandman's Wedding

Though George Parker's name is not formally attached to this "Cantata" there would appear little doubt, from internal evidence, that it, with the two songs immediately following, forms part of a characteristic series from the pen of this roving soldier-actor. Parker was born in 1732 at Green Street, near Canterbury and was 'early admitted', he says, 'to walk the quarterdeck as a midshipman on board the Falmouth and the Guernsey'. A series of youthful indiscretions in London obliged him to leave the navy, and in or about 1754 to enlist as a common soldier in the 20th regiment of foot, the second battalion of which became in 1758 the 67th regiment, under the command of Wolfe. In his regiment he continued a private, corporal, and

sergeant for seven years, was present at the
siege of Belleisle, and saw service in Portugal,
Gibraltar, and Minorca. At the end of the war
he returned home as a supernumerary excise-
man. About 1761 his friends placed him in the
King's Head inn at Canterbury where he soon
failed. Parker went upon the stage in Ire-
land, and in company with Brownlow Ford, a
clergyman of convivial habits, strolled over the
greater part of the island. On his return to London he played several times at the Haymarket,
and was later introduced by Goldsmith to Colman.
But on account of his corpulence Colman de-
clined his services. Parker then joined the pro-
vincial strolling companies, and was engaged for
one season with Digges, then manager of the
Edinburgh Theatre. At Edinburgh he married an
actress named Heydon, from whom, however, he
was soon obliged to part on account of her
dissolute life. Returning again to London, he
set up as wandering lecturer on elocution, and
in this character travelled with varying success
through England. In November 1776 he set
out on a visit to France, and lived at Paris for
upwards of six months on funds supplied by his
father. His resources being exhausted, he left
Paris in the middle of July 1777 on foot.
On reaching England he made another lecturing
tour, which proved unsuccessful. His wit, humour,
and knowledge of the world rendered him at one
time an indispensable appendage to convivial
gatherings of a kind; but in his later days he
was so entirely neglected as to be obliged to sell
gingerbread-nuts at fairs and race-meetings for a
subsistance. He died in Coventry poorhouse in
April 1800.

The Happy Pair

and

The Bunter's Christening

and

The Masqueraders

See note (*ante*) to "The Sandman's Wedding".
Life's Painter etc. ran through several editions.

The Flash Man of St. Giles

Stanza II, line 7. *Drunk as David's sow*=beastly
drunk.   Grose (*Classical Dictionary of the Vulgar
Tongue*) says: One David Lloyd, a Welshman, who
kept an ale-house at Hereford, had a sow with six
legs, which was an object of great curiosity.   One
day David's wife, having indulged too freely, lay
down in the sty to sleep, and a company coming
to see the sow, David led them to the sty, saying,
as usual, "There is a sow for you! Did you
ever see the like?"   One of the visitors replied,
"Well, it is the drunkenest sow I ever beheld."
Whence the woman was ever after called "Davy's
sow."

A Leary Mot

Stanza III, line 1. *Cock and Hen Club* = a
free-and-easy for both sexes.
Stanza IV, line 4. *Tom Cribb—see* note p. 223.

"The Night Before Larry was Stretched"

Neither the authorship nor the date of these inimitable verses are definitely known. According to the best authorities, Will Maher, a shoemaker of Waterford, wrote the song. Dr. Robert Burrowes, Dean of St. Finbar's Cork, to whom it has been so often attributed, certainly did not. Often quoted in song book and elsewhere. Francis Sylvester Mahony, better known as "Father Prout" contributed to *Fraser's Magazine* the following translation into the French.

La mort de Socrate.

Par l'Abbé de Prout, Curé du Mont-aux-Cressons,
près de Cork.

A la veille d'être pendu,
Notr' Laurent reçut dans son gîte,
    Honneur qui lui était bien dû,
De nombreux amis la visite;
    Car chacun scavait que Laurent
A son tour rendrait la pareille,
    Chapeau montre, et veste engageant,
Pour que l'ami put boire bouteille,
    Ni faire, à gosier sec, le saut.

"Helas, notre garçon!" lui dis-je,
"Combien je regrette ton sort!
    Te voilà fleur, que sur sa tige
Moisonne la cruelle mort!" —
    "Au diable," dit-il, "le roi George!
Ça me fait la valeur d'un bouton;
    Devant le boucher qui m'égorge,
Je serai comme un doux mouton,
    Et saurai montrer du courage!"

Des amis déjà la cohorte
Remplissait son étroit réduit:
    Six chandelles, ho! qu'on apporte,
Donnons du lustre à cette nuit!
    Alors je cherchai à connaître
S'il s'était dûment repenti?
    "Bah! c'est les fourberies des prêtres
Les gredins, ils en ont menti,
    Et leurs contes d'enfer sont faux!"

    L'on demande les cartes. Au jeu
Laurent voit un larron qui triche;
    D'honneur tout rempli, il prend feu,
Et du bon coup de poign l'affiche.
    "Ha, coquin! de mon dernier jour
Tu croyais profiter, peut-être;
    Tu oses me jouer ce tour!
Prends ça pour ta peine, vil traître!
    Et apprends à te bien conduire!"

    Quand nous eûmes cessé nos ébats,
Laurent, en ce triste repaire
    Pour le disposer au trépas,
Voit entrer Monsieur le Vicaire.
    Après un sinistre regard,
Le front de sa main il se frotte,
    Disant tout haut, "Venez plus tard!"
Et tout bas, "Vilaine calotte!"
    Puis son verre il vida deux fois.

    Lors il parla de l'échaufaud,
Et de sa dernière cravate;
    Grands dieux! que ça paraissait beau
De la voir mourir en Socrate!
    Le trajet en chantant il fit --
La chanson point ne fut un pseaume;
    Mais palit un peu quand il vit
La statute de Roy Guillaume —
    Les pendards n'aiment pas ce roi!

Quand fut au bout de son voyage,
Le gibet fut prêt en un clin:
Mourant il tourna de visage
Vers la bonne ville de Dublin.
Il dansa la carmagnole,
Et mourit comme fit Malbrouck;
Puis nous enterrâmes le drôle
Au cimetière de Donnybrook
Que son âme y soit en repos!

Stanza V, line 3. *Kilmainham*, a gaol near Dublin.

Stanza VI, line 7. *King William*, the statute of William III erected on College Green in commemoration of the Battle of the Boyne. It was long the object of much contumely on the part of the Nationalists. It was blown to pieces in 1836, but was subsequently restored.

The Song of the Young Prig

Said to have been written by Little Arthur Chambers, the Prince of Prigs, who was one of the most expert thieves of his time. He began to steal when he was in petticoats, and died a short time before Jack Sheppard came into notice. Internal evidence, however, renders this attributed authorship very improbable.

Stanza I, line 1. *Dyot's Isle, i.e.,* Dyot St., St. Giles, afterwards called George St. Bloomsbury, was a well-known rookery where thieves and their associates congregated.

Stanza II, line 3. *And I my reading learnt betime From studying pocket-books.* "Pocket-book" = *reader.*

Stanza IV, line 1. *To work capital* = to commit a crime punishable with death. Previous to 1829 many offences, now thought comparatively trivial, were deemed to merit the extreme penalty of the law.

The Milling Match

Tom Cribb's Memorial to Congress : With a Preface, Notes, and Appendix. By One of the Fancy. London, Longmans & Co., 1819. There were several editions. Usually, with good reason, ascribed to Thomas Moore. It may be remarked that, though the Irish Anacreon's claim to fame rests avowedly on his more serious contributions to literature, he was, nevertheless, never so popular as when dealing with what, in the early part of the present century, was known as THE FANCY. Pugilism then took the place, in the popular mind, that football and cricket now occupy. Tom Cribb was born at Hanham in the parish of Bitton, Gloucestershire, in 1781, and coming to London at the age of thirteen followed the trade of a bell-hanger, then became a porter at the public wharves, and was afterwards a sailor. From the fact of his having worked as a coal porter he became known as the 'Black Diamond,' and under this appellation he fought his first public battle against George Maddox at Wood Green on 7 Jan. 1805, when after seventy-six rounds he was proclaimed the victor, and received much praise for his coolness and temper under very unfair treatment. In 1807 he was introduced to Captain Barclay, who, quickly perceiving his natural good qualities, took him in hand, and trained him under his own eye. He won the championship from Bob Gregson in 1808 but in 1809 he was beaten by Jem Belcher. He subsequently regained the

belt. After an unsuccessful venture as a coal
merchant at Hungerford Wharf, London, he
underwent the usual metamorphosis from a pugilist
to a publican, and took the Golden Lion in Southwark; but finding this position too far eastward
for his aristocratic patrons he removed to the
King's Arms at the corner of Duke Street and
King Street, St. James's, and subsequently, in 1828,
to the Union Arms, 26 Panton Street, Haymarket.
On 24 Jan. 1821 it was decided that Cribb,
having held the championship for nearly ten years
without receiving a challenge, ought not to be
expected to fight any more, and was to be per-
mitted to hold the title of champion for the
remainder of his life. On the day of the coronation of George IV, Cribb, dressed as a page, was
among the prizefighters engaged to guard the
entrance to Westminster Hall. His declining years
were disturbed by domestic troubles and severe
pecuniary losses, and in 1839 he was obliged to
give up the Union Arms to his creditors. He
died in the house of his son, a baker in the High
Street, Woolwich, on 11 May 1848, aged 67, and
was buried in Woolwich churchyard, where, in
1851, a monument representing a lion grieving
over the ashes of a hero was erected to his memory. As a professor of his art he was matchless, and in his observance of fair play he was
never excelled; he bore a character of unim-
peachable integrity and unquestionable humanity.

Ya-Hip, My Hearties!

Stanza III, line 8. *Houyhnhnms.* A race of
horses endowed with human reason, and bearing
rule over the race of man—a reference to Dean
Swift's *Gulliver's Travels* (1726).

Sonnets for The Fancy

Pierce Egan, the author of the adventures of Tom and Jerry was born about 1772 and died in 1849. He had won his spurs as a sporting reporter by 1812, and for eleven years was recognised as one of the smartest of the epigrammatists, song-writers, and wits of the time. *Boxiana*, a monthly serial, was commenced in 1818. It consisted of 'Sketches of Modern Pugilism', giving memoirs and portraits of all the most celebrated pugilists, contemporary and antecedent, with full reports of their respective prize-fights, victories, and defeats, told with so much spirited humour, yet with such close attention to accuracy, that the work holds a unique position. It was continued in several volumes, with copperplates, to 1824. At this date, having seen that Londoners read with avidity his accounts of country sports and pastimes, he conceived the idea of a similar description of the amusements pursued by sporting men in town. Accordingly he announced the publication of *Life in London* in shilling numbers, monthly, and secured the aid of George Cruikshank, and his brother, Isaac Robert Cruikshank to draw and engrave the illustrations in aquatint, to be coloured by hand. George IV had caused Egan to be presented at court, and at once accepted the dedication of the forthcoming work. This was the more generous on the king's part because he must have known himself to have been often satirised and caricatured mercilessly in the *Green Bag* literature by G. Cruikshank, the intended illustrator. On 15 July 1821 appeared the first number of *Life in London;* or, 'The Day and Night Scenes of Jerry Hawthorn, Esq., and his elegant friend, Corinthian Jem, accompanied by Bob Logic, the Oxonian, in their Rambles and Sprees through the Metropolis.' The success was instantaneous and unprecedented. It took both town and country by storm. So great was the demand for copies, increasing with the publication of each successive number, month by month, that the colourists could not keep pace with the printers. The alternate scenes of high life and low life, the contrasted characters, and revelations of misery side by side with prodigal waste and folly, attracted attention, while the vivacity of dialogue and description never flagged.

Stanza III, line 10. *New Drop.* The extreme penalty of the law, long carried out at Tyburn (near the Marble Arch corner of Hyde Park), was ultimately transferred to Newgate. The lament for " Tyburn's merry roam " was, without doubt, heart-felt and characteristic. Executions were then one of the best of all good excuses for a picnic and jollification. Yet the change of scene to Newgate does not appear to have detracted much from these functions as shows. " Newgate to-day," says a recent writer in *The Daily Mail*, is little wanted, and all but vacant, as a general rule. In former days enormous crowds were herded together indiscriminately— young and old, innocent and guilty, men, women, and children, the heinous offender, and the neophyte in crime. The worst part of the prison was the " Press Yard," the place then allotted to convicts cast for death. There were as many as sixty or seventy sometimes within these narrow limits, and most were kept six months and more thus hovering between a wretched existence and a shameful death. Men in momentary expectation of being hanged rubbed shoulders with others still hoping for reprieve. If the first were seriously inclined, they were quite debarred from private religious meditation, but consorted, perforce, with reckless ruffians, who played leap-frog, and swore and drank continually. Infants of tender years were among the condemned; lunatics, too, raged furiously through the Press Yard, and were a constant annoyance and danger to all. The "condemned sermon" in the prison chapel drew a crowd of fashionable folk, to stare at those who were to die, packed together in a long pew hung with black, and on a table in front was placed an open coffin. Outside, in the Old Bailey, on the days of execution, the awful scenes nearly baffle description. Thousands collected to gloat over the dying struggles of the criminals, and fought and roared and trampled each other to death in their horrible eagerness, so that hundreds were wounded or killed. Ten or a dozen were sometimes hanged in a row, men and women side by side.

The True Bottomed Boxer

The Universal Songster, or Museum of Mirth: forming the most complete collection of ancient and modern songs in the English language, with a classified Index ... Embellished with a Frontispiece and wood cuts, designed by George Cruikshank etc. 3vols. London, 1825-26. 8vo.

Stanza I, line 1. *Moulsey-Hurst rig* = a prizefight: Moulsey-Hurst, near Hampton Court, was long a favorite *venue* for pugilistic encounters. Line 3. *Fibbing a nob is most excellent gig* = getting in a quick succession of blows on the head is good fun. Line 4. *Kneading the dough* = a good pummelling. Line 6. *Belly-go-firsters* =

an initial blow, generally given in the stomach. Line 8. *Measuring mugs for a chancery job* = getting the head under the arm or 'in chancery'.

Stanza II, line 1. *Flooring* = downing (a man). *Flushing* = delivering a blow right on the mark, and straight from the shoulder. Line 5. *Crossing* = unfair fighting; shirking.

Stanza III, line 5. *Victualling-office* = the stomach. Line 6. *Smeller and ogles* = nose and eyes. Line 7. *Bread-basket* = stomach. Line 8. *In twig* = in form; ready.

Bobby and His Mary

[See *ante* for note on *Universal Songster*].

Stanza I, line 1. *Dyot Street*, see note page 222.

Stanza II, line 16. *St. Pulchre's bell*, the great bell of St. Sepulchre's Holborn, close to Newgate, always begins to toll a little before the hour of execution, under the bequest of Richard Dove, who directed that an exhortation should be made to ".... prisoners that are within, Who for wickedness and sin are appointed to die, Give ear unto this passing bell."

Poor Luddy

Thomas John Dibdin (1771—1841), the author of this song, was an actor and dramatist —an illegitimate son of Charles Dibdin the elder. He claimed to have written nearly 2000 songs.

The Pickpocket's Chaunt

Eugene François Vidocq was a native of Arras, where his father was a baker. From early associations he fell into courses of excess which led to his flying from the paternal roof. After various, rapid, and unexampled events in the romance of real life, in which he was everything by turns and nothing long, he was liberated from prison, and became the principal and most active agent of police. He was made chief of the Police de Sureté under Messrs. Delavau and Franchet, and continued in that capacity from the year 1810 till 1827, during which period he extirpated the most formidable gangs of ruffians to whom the excesses of the revolution and subsequent events had given full scope for daring robberies and iniquitous excesses. He settled down as a paper manufacturer at St. Mandé near Paris.

Of Maginn (1793—1842) it may be said he was, without question, one of the most versatile writers of his time. He is, perhaps, best remembered in connection with the *Noctes Ambrosianæ,* which first appeared in *Blackwood,* and with the idea of which Maginn is generally credited. He was also largely concerned with the inception of *Fraser's.* Maginn's English rendering of Vidocq's famous song first appeared in *Blackwood* for July 1829. For the benefit of the curious the original is appended. It will be seen that Maginn was very faithful to his copy.

En roulant de vergne en vergne [1]
Pour apprendre à goupiner, [2]
J'ai rencontré la mercandière, [3]
Lonfa malura dondaine,
Qui du pivois solisait, [4]
Lonfa malura dondé.

J'ai rencontré la mercandière
Qui du pivois solisait;
Je lui jaspine en bigorne; [5]
Lonfa malura dondaine,
Qu'as tu donc à morfiller? [6]
Lonfa malura dondé.

Je lui jaspine en bigorne;
Qu'as tu donc à morfiller?
J'ai du chenu [7] pivois sans lance. [8]
Lonfa malura dondaine,
Et du larton savonné [9]
Lonfa malura dondé.

J'ai du chenu pivois sans lance
Et du larton savonné,
Une lourde, [10] une tournante, [11]
Lonfa malura dondaine,
Et un pieu [12] pour roupiller [13]
Lonfa malura dondé.

Une lourde, une tournante
Et un pieu pour roupiller.
J'enquille [14] dans sa cambriole, [15]
Lonfa malura dondaine,
Espérant de l'entifler, [16]
Lonfa malura dondé.

[1] Vergne, *town.*
[2] Goupiner, *to steal.*
[3] Mercandière, *tradeswomen.*
[4] Du pivois solisait, *sold wine.*
[5] Jaspine en bigorne, *say in cant.*
[6] Morfiller. *to eat and drink.*
[7] Chenu, *good.*
    Lance, *water.*
[9] Larton savonné, *white bread.*
[10] Lourde, *door.*
[11] Tournante, *key.*
[12] Pieu, *bed.*
[13] Roupiller, *to sleep.*
[14] J'enquille, *I enter.*
[15] Cambriole, *room.*
[16] Entifler, *to marry.*

J'enquille dans sa cambriole
Espérant de l'entifler;
Je rembroque [1] au coin du rifle, [2]
Lonfa malura dondaine,
Un messière [3] qui pionçait, [4]
Lonfa malura dondé.

Je rembroque au coin du rifle
Un messière qui pionçait;
J'ai sondé dans ses vallades, [5]
Lonfa malura dondaine,
Son carle [6] j'ai pessigué, [7]
Lonfa malura dondé.

J'ai sondé dans ses vallades,
Son carle j'ai pessigué,
Son carle et sa tocquante, [8]
Lonfa malura dondaine,
Et ses attaches de cé, [9]
Lonfa malura dondé.

Son carle et sa tocquante,
Et ses attaches de cé,
Son coulant [10] et sa montante, [11]
Lonfa malura dondaine,
Et son combre galuché [12]
Lonfa malura dondé.

Son coulant et sa montante
Et son combre galuché,
Son frusque, [13] aussi sa lisette, [14]
Lonfa malura dondaine,
Et ses tirants brodanchés, [15]
Lonfa malura dondé.

---

[1] Rembroque, *see*.
[2] Rifle, *fire*.
[3] Mosisère, *man*.
[4] Pionçait, *was sleeping*.
[5] Vallades, *pockets*.
[6] Carle, *money*.
[7] Pessigué, *taken*.
[8] Tocquante, *watch*.
[9] Attaches de cé, *silver buckles*.
[10] Coulant, *chain*.
[11] Montante, *breeches*.
[12] Combre galuché, *laced hat*.
[13] Frusque, *coat*.
[14] Lisette, *waistcoat*.
[15] Tirants brodanchés, *embroidered stockings*.

Son frusque, aussi sa lisette
Et ses tirants brodanchés.
Crompe, [1] crompe, mercandière,
Lonfa malura dondaine,
Car nous serions béquillés, [2]
Lonfa malura dondé.

Crompe, crompe, mercandière,
Car nous serions béquillés.
Sur la placarde de vergne, [3]
Lonfa malura dondaine,
Il nous faudrait gambiller, [4]
Lonfa malura dondé.

Sur la placarde de vergne
Il nous faudrait gambiller,
Allumés [5] de toutes ces largues, [6]
Lonfa malura dondaine,
Et du trèpe [7] rassemblé,
Lonfa malura dondé.

Allumés de toutes ces largues
Et du trèpe rassemblé;
Et de ces charlots bons drilles, [8]
Lonfa malura dondaine,
Tous aboulant [9] goupiner.
Lonfa malura dondé.

Stanza XIII, line 5. Cotton, the ordinary at
Newgate.

[1] Crompe, *run away.*
[2] Béquillés, *hanged.*
[3] Placarde de vergne, *public place.*
[4] Gambiller, *to dance.*
[5] Allumés, *stared at.*
[6] Largues, *women.*
[7] Trèpe, *crowd.*
[8] Charlots bons drilles, *jolly thieves.*
[9] Aboulant, *coming.*

On the Prigging Lay

H. T. R., the English translator of Vidocq's
Memoirs (4 vol., 1828-9), says of this and the
following renderings from the French that they
"with all their faults and all their errors, are to
be added to the list of the translator's sins, who
would apologise to the Muse did he but know
which of the nine presides over Slang poetry."
The original of "On the Prigging Lay" is as
follows:—

Un jour à la Croix-Rouge
Nous étions dix à douze
    (*She interrupted herself with* "Comme
    à l'instant même.")
Nous étions dix à douze
Tous grinches de renom, [1]
Nous attendions la sorgue [2]
Voulant poisser des bogues [3]
Pour faire du billon. [4] (*bis*)

Partage ou non partage
Tout est à notre usage;
N'épargnons le poitou [5]
Poissons avec adresse [6]
Messières et gonzesses [7]
Sans faire de regout. [8] (*bis*)

Dessus le pont au change
Certain argent-de-change
Se criblait au charron, [9]
J'engantai sa toquante [10]
Ses attaches brillantes [11]
Avec ses billemonts. [12] (*bis*)

[1] Thieves.
[2] Night.
[3] Watches.
[4] Money.
[5] Let us be cautious.
[6] Let us rob.
[7] Citizen and wife.
[8] Awaken suspicion.
[9] Cried "Thief."
[10] I took his watch.
[11] His diamond buckles.
[12] His bank notes.

Quand douze plombes crossent, [1]
Ses pegres s'en retournant [2]
Au tapis de Montron [3]
Montron ouvre ta lourde, [4]
Si tu veux que j'aboule, [5]
Et piausse en ton bocsin. [6]   (*bis*)

Montron drogue à sa larque, [7]
Bonnis-moi donc girofle [8]
Qui sont ces pegres-là ? [9]
Des grinchisseurs de bogues, [10]
Esquinteurs de boutoques, [11]
Les connobres tu pas ? [12]   (*bis*)

Et vite ma culbute ; [13]
Quand je vois mon affure [14]
Je suis toujours paré [15]
Du plus grand coeur du monde
Je vais à la profonde [16]
Pour vous donner du frais. (*bis*)

Mais déjà la patrarque, [17]
Au clair de la moucharde, [18]
Nous reluge de loin. [19]
L'aventure est étrange,
C'était l'argent-de-change,
Que suivait les roussins. [20]   (*bis*)

[1] Twelve oclock strikes.
[2] The thieves.
[3] At the cabaret.
[4] Your door.
[5] Give money.
[6] Sleep at your house.
[7] Asks his wife.
[8] Say, my love.
[9] These thieves.
[10] Watch stealers.
[11] Burglars.
[12] Do you not know them?
[13] Breeches.
[14] Profit.
[15] Ready.
[16] Cellar.
[17] Patrol.
[18] The moon.
[19] Looks at us.
[20] Spies.

A des fois l'on rigole [1]
Ou bien l'on pavillonne [2]
Qu'on devrait lansquiner [3]
Raille, griviers, et cognes [4]
Nous ont pour la cigogne [5]
Tretons marrons paumés. [6]   (*bis*)

The Lag's Lament

See Note *ante*, "On the Prigging Lay". The
original runs as follows:—

Air: *L'Heureux Pilote.*

Travaillant d'ordinaire,
La sorgue dans Pantin, [7]
Dans mainte et mainte affaire
Faisant très-bon choppin, [8]
Ma gente cambriote, [9]
Rendoublée de camelotte, [10]
De la dalle au flaquet; [11]
Je vivais sans disgrace,
Sans regout ni morace, [12]
Sans taff et sans regret. [13]

J'ai fait par comblance [14]
Giroude larguecapé, [15]
Soiffant picton sans lance, [16]
Pivois non maquillé, [17]
Tirants, passe à la rousse, [18]
Attachés de gratouse, [19]

[1] Laughs.
[2] Jokes.
[3] To weep.
[4] Exempt, soldiers and gendarmes.
[5] Palace of justice.
[6] Taken in the act.
[7] Evening in Paris.
[8] A good booty.
[9] Chamber.
[10] Full of goods.
[11] Money in the pocket.
[12] Without fear or uneasiness.
[13] Without care.
[14] An increase.
[15] A handsome mistress.
[16] Drinking wine without water.
[17] Unadulterated wine.
[18] Stockings.
[19] Lace.

Combriot galuché. [1]
Cheminant en bon drille,
Un jour à la Courtille
Je m'en étais enganté. [2]

En faisant nos gambades,
Un grand messière franc, [3]
Voulant faire parade,
Serre un bogue d'orient. [4]
Après la gambriade, [5]
Le filant sur l'estrade, [6]
D'esbrouf je l'estourbis, [7]
J'enflaque sa limace, [8]
Son bogue, ses frusques, ses passes, [9]
Je m'en fus au fourallis. [10]

Par contretemps, ma largue,
Voulant se piquer d'honneur,
Craignant que je la nargue
Moi que n' suis pas taffeur, [11]
Pour gonfler ses valades
Encasque dans un rade [12]
Sert des sigues a foison [13]
On la crible à la grive, [14]
Je m' la donne et m' esquive, [15]
Elle est pommée maron. [16]

Le quart d'oeil lui jabotte [17]
Mange sur tes nonneurs, [18]
Lui tire une carotte
Lui montant la couleur. [19]

[1] Laced hat.
[2] Clad.
[3] Citizen.
[4] A gold watch.
[5] Dance.
[6] Following him in the boulevard.
[7] I stun him.
[8] I take off his shirt.
[9] I steal his watch, clothes and shoes.
[10] The receiving house.
[11] Coward.
[12] Enters a shop.
[13] Steals money.
[14] They call for the guard.
[15] I fly.
[16] Taken in the fact.
[17] The commissary questions him.
[18] Denounces his accomplices.
[19] Tell a falsehood.

L'on vient, on me ligotte, [1]
Adieu, ma cambriote,
Mon beau pieu, mes dardants [2]
Je monte à la cigogne, [3]
On me gerbe à la grotte, [4]
Au tap et pour douze ans. [5]

    Ma largue n' sera plus gironde,
Je serais vioc aussi; [6]
Faudra pour plaire au monde,
Clinquant, frusque, maquis. [7]
Tout passe dans la tigne, [8]
Et quoiqu'on en juspine. [9]
C'est un f— flanchet, [10]
Douze longes de tirade, [11]
Pour un rigolade, [12]
Pour un moment d'attrait.

Stanza II, line 2. *So gay, so nutty and so knowing*—See *Don Juan*, Canto XI, stanza ...

Stanza VI, line 1. Sir Richard Birnie the chief magistrate at Bow St.

"Nix my Doll, Pals, Fake Away"

Ainsworth in his preface to *Rookwood* makes the following remarks on this and the three following songs:—"As I have casually alluded to the flash song of Jerry Juniper, I may be allowed to make a few observations upon this branch of versification. It is somewhat curious with a dialect so

---

[1] They tie me.
[2] My fine bed, my loves.
[3] The dock.
[4] They condemn my to the galleys.
[5] To exposure.
[6] Old.
[7] Rouge.
[8] In this world.
[9] Whatever people say.
[10] Lot.
[11] Twelve years of letters.
[12] Fool.

racy, idiomatic, and plastic as our own cant, that its metrical capabilities should have been so little essayed. The French have numerous *chansons d'argot*, ranging from the time of Charles Bourdigné and Villon down to that of Vidocq and Victor Hugo, the last of whom has enlivened the horrors of his *'Dernier Jour d'un Condamné'* by a festive song of this class. The Spaniards possess a large collection of *Romances de Germania*, by various authors, amongst whom Quevedo holds a distinguished place. We on the contrary, have scarcely any slang songs of merit. This barreness is not attributable to the poverty of the soil, but to the want of due cultivation. Materials are at hand in abundance, but there have been few operators. Dekker, Beaumont and Fletcher, and Ben Jonson, have all dealt largely in this jargon, but not lyrically; and one of the earliest and best specimens of a canting-song occurs in Brome's *'Jovial Crew;'* and in the *'Adventures of Bamfylde Moore Carew'* there is a solitary ode addressed by the mendicant fraternity to their newly-elected monarch; but it has little humour, and can scarcely be called a genuine canting-song. This ode brings us down to our own time; to the effusions of the illustrious Pierce Egan; to Tom Moore's Flights of *'Fancy;'* to John Jackson's famous chant, *'On the High Toby Spice flash the Muzzle,'* cited by Lord Byron in a note to *'Don Juan;'* and to the glorious Irish ballad, worth them all put together, entitled *'The Night before Larry was stretched.'* This is attributed to the late Dean Burrowes, of Cork. [*See* Note, p. 220 *Ed.*]. It is worthy of note, that almost all modern aspirants to the graces of the *Musa Pedestris* are Irishmen. Of all rhymesters of the *'Road,'* however, Dean Burrowes is, as yet, most fully entitled to the laurel. Larry is quite 'the potato!'

"I venture to affirm that I have done something more than has been accomplished by my predecessors, or contemporaries, with the significant language under consideration. I have written *a purely flash song ;* of which the great and peculiar merit consists in its being utterly incomprehensible to the uninformed understanding, while its meaning must be perfectly clear and perspicuous to the practised *patterer* of *Romany,* or *Pedler's French.* I have, moreover, been the first to introduce and naturalize amongst us a measure which, though common enough in the Argotic minstrelsy of France, has been hitherto utterly unknown to our *pedestrian* poetry." How mistaken Ainsworth was in his claim, thus ambiguously preferred, the present volume shows. Some years after the song alluded to, better known under the title of '*Nix my dolly, pals,—fake away !*' sprang into extraordinary popularity, being set to music by Rodwell, and chanted by glorious Paul Bedford and clever little Mrs. Keeley.

The Game of High Toby
and
The Double Cross

See note to "Nix my Doll, Pals, etc.," *ante.*

The House Breaker's Song

G. W. M. Reynolds followed closely on the heels of Dickens when the latter scored his great success in *The Pickwick Papers.* He was a most voluminous scribbler, but none of his productions are of high literary merit.

The Faking Boy to the Crap is gone
The Nutty Blowen
The Faker's New Toast

and

My Mother

" Bon Gualtier " was the joint *nom-de-plume* of W. E. Aytoun and Sir Theodore Martin. Between 1840 and 1844 they worked together in the production of *The Bon Gualtier Ballads*, which acquired such great popularity that thirteen large editions of them were called for between 1855 and 1877. They were also associated at this time in writing many prose magazine articles of a humorous character, as well as a series of translations of Goethe's ballads and minor poems, which, after appearing in *Blackwood's Magazine*, were some years afterwards (1858) collected and published in a volume. The four pieces above mentioned appeared as stated in *Taits Edinburgh Magazine* under the title of "Flowers of Hemp, or the Newgate Garland," and are parodies of well-known songs.

The High Pad's Frolic

and

The Dashy, Splashy.... Little Stringer

Leman Rede (1802-47) an author of numerous successful dramatic pieces, and a contributor to the weekly and monthly journals of the day, chiefly to the *New Monthly* and *Bentley's*. He was born in Hamburgh, his father a barrister.

Some of the best parts ever played by Liston, John Reeve, Charles Mathews, Keeley, and G. Wild were written by him.

The Bould Yeoman

The Bridle-cull and his little Pop-gun

Jack Flashman

Miss Dolly Trull

and

The By-blow of the Jug

See Note to "Sonnets for The Fancy" p. 225. Captain Macheath was one of Egan's latest, and by no means one of his best, productions. It is now very scarce.

The Cadger's Ball

John Labern, a once popular, but now forgotten music-hall artiste, and song-writer, issued several collections of the songs of the day. It is from one of these that "The Cadger's Ball" is taken.

"Dear Bill, This Stone-Jug"

The state of affairs described in this poem is now happily a thing of the past. Newgate, as a prison, has almost ceased to be. Only when the Courts are sitting do its functions commence, and then there is constant coming and going between the old city gaol and the real London prison of to-day, Holloway Castle.

The Leary Man

The Vulgar Tongue, by Ducange Anglicus, is, as a glossary, of no account whatever; the only thing not pilfered from Brandon's *Poverty, Mendicity, and Crime* being this song. Where that came from deponent knoweth not.

A Hundred Stretches Hence

The Rogue's Lexicon, mainly reprinted from Grose's *Dictionary of the Vulgar Tongue*, is of permanent interest and value to the philologist and student for the many curious survivals of, and strange shades of meaning occuring in, slang words and colloquilisms after transplantation to the States. G. W. Matsell was for a time the chief of the New York police.

The Chickaleary Cove

Vance, a music-hall singer and composer in the sixties, made his first great hit in *Jolly Dogs; or Slap-bang! here we are again.* This was followed by *The Chickaleary Cove:* a classic in its way.

'Arry at a Political Picnic

The 'Arry Ballads' are too fresh in public memory to need extensive quotation. The example given is a fair sample of the series; which, taken as a whole, very cleverly "hit off" the idiosyncrasies and foibles of the London larrikin.

Stanza VIII, line 4. *Walker* = Be off!

"Rum Coves that Relieve us"

Heinrich Baumann, the author of *Londonismen*, an English-German glossary of cant and slang, to which "Rum Coves that Relieve us" forms the preface.

Villon's Good Night
Villon's Straight Tip

and

Culture in the Slums

William Ernest Henley, poet, critic, dramatist, and editor was born at Gloucester in 1849, and educated at the same city. In his early years (says *Men of the Time*) he suffered much from ill-health, and the first section of his *Book of Verses* (1888: 4th ed. 1893), *In Hospital: Rhymes and Rhythms,* was a record of experiences in the Old Infirmary, Edinburgh, in 1873-5. In 1875 he began writing for the London magazines, and in 1877 was one of the founders as well as the editor of *London.* In this journal much of his early verse appeared. He was afterwards appointed editor of *The Magazine of Art,* and in 1889 of *The Scots,* afterwards *The National Observer.* To these journals, as well as to *The Athenæum* and *Saturday Review* he has contributed many critical articles, a selection of which was published in 1890 under the title of *Views and Reviews.* In collaboration with Robert Louis Stevenson he has published a volume of plays, one of which, *Beau Austin,* was produced at the Haymarket Theatre in 1892. His second volume of verses—*The Song of the Sword*—marks a new departure in style. He has edited a fine col-

16

lection of verses, *Lyra Heroica*, and, with Mr. Charles Whibley, an anthology of English prose. In 1893 Mr. Henley received the honour of an L.L.D. degree of St. Andrew's university. At the present time he is also editing *The New Review*, a series of *Tudor Translations*, a new *Byron*, a new *Burns*, and collaborating with Mr. J. S. Farmer in *Slang and its Analogues;* an historical dictionary of slang.

" *Villon's Straight Tip :* Stanza I, line 1. *Screeve =* provide (or work with) begging-letters. Line 2. *Fake the broads* = pack the cards. *Fig a nag =* play the coper with an old horse and a fig of ginger. Line 3. *Knap a yack* = steal a watch. Line 4. *Pitch a snide* = pass a false coin. *Smash a rag* = change a false note. Line 5. *Duff =* sell sham smugglings. *Nose and lag* = collect evidence for the police. Line 6. *Get the straight =* get the office, and back a winner. Line 7. *Multy* (expletive) = " bloody ". Line 8. *Booze and the blowens cop the lot:* cf. " 'Tis all to taverns and to lasses." (A. Lang).

Stanza II, line 1. *Fiddle* = swindle. *Fence =* deal in stolen goods. *Mace* = welsh. *Mack =* pimp. Line 2. *Moskeneer* = to pawn for more than the pledge is worth. *Flash the drag* = wear women's clothes for an improper purpose. Line 3. *Dead-lurk a crib* = house-break in church time. *Do a crack* = burgle with violence. Line 4. *Pad with a slang* = tramp with a show. Line 5. *Mump and gag* = beg and talk. Line 6. *Tats =* dice. *Spot*, (at billiards). Line 7. *Stag* = shilling.

Stanza III, line 2. *Flash your flag* = sport your apron. Line 4. *Mug* = make faces. Line 5. *Nix* = nothing. Line 6. *Graft* = trade. Line 7. *Goblins* = sovereigns. *Stravag* = go astray.

The Moral. Line 1. *Up the spout and Charley Wag* = expressions of dispersal. Line 2. *Wipes* = handkerchiefs. *Tickers* = watches. Line 3. *Squeezer* = halter. *Scrag* = neck.

"Tottie"

A Plank-Bed Ballad

and

The Rondeau of the Knock

G. R. Sims ("Dagonet") needs little introduction to present-day readers. Born in London in 1847, he was educated at Hanwell College, and afterwards at Bonn. He joined the staff of *Fun* on the death of Tom Hood the younger in 1874, and *The Weekly Despatch* the same year. Since 1877 he has been a contributor to *The Referee* under the pseudonym of "Dagonet". A voluminous miscellaneous writer, dramatist, poet, and novelist, M. Sims shows yet no diminution of his versatility and power.

Wot Cher!

Our Little Nipper

and

The Coster's Serenade

Albert Chevalier, a "coster poet", music-hall artist, and musician of French extraction was born in Hammersmith. He is a careful, competent actor of minor parts, and sings his own little ditties extremely well.

APPENDIX.

THERE are still one or two "waifs and strays" to be mentioned:—

I.

In *Don Juan,* canto XI, stanzas xvii—xix, Byron thus describes one of his *dramatis personæ.*

Poor Tom was once a kiddy upon town,
  A thorough varmint and a real swell...
Full flash, all fancy, until fairly diddled,
His pockets first, and then his body riddled.

*   *   *   *   *   *   *   *   *

He from the world had cut off a great man
  Who in his time had made heroic bustle.
Who in a row like Tom could lead the van,
Booze in the ken, or in the spellken hustle?
  Who queer a flat? Who (spite of Bow Street's
                                        ban)
  On the high-toby-splice so flash the muzzle?
Who on a lark, with Black-eyed Sal (his blowing)
So prime, so swell, so nutty, and so knowing?

In a note Byron says, "The advance of science and of language has rendered it unnecessary to translate the above good and true English, spoken

in its original purity by the select mobility and
their patrons. The following is the stanza of a
song which was very popular, at least in my
early days:—

("If there be any German so ignorant as to
require a traduction, I refer him to my old friend
and corporeal pastor and master John Jackson,
Esq., Professor of Pugilism.")

On the high toby splice flash the muzzle
    In spite of each gallows old scout;
If you at the spellken can't hustle
    You'll be hobbled in making a clout.
Then your blowing will wax gallows haughty,
    When she hears of your scaly mistake
She'll surely turn snitch for the forty—
    That her Jack may be regular weight.

John Jackson, to whom is attributed the slang
song of which the foregoing stanza is a fragment
was the son of a London builder. He was born
in London on 28 Sept. 1769, and though he
fought but thrice, was champion of England from
1795 to 1803, when he retired, and was succeeded
by Belcher. After leaving the prize-ring, Jackson
established a school at No. 13 Bond Street, where
he gave instructions in the art of self-defence,
and was largely patronised by the nobility of
the day. At the coronation of George IV he
was employed, with eighteen other prize-fighters
dressed as pages, to guard the entrance to Westminster Abbey and Hall. He seems, according
to the inscription on a mezzotint engraving by
C. Turner, to have subsequently been landlord of
the Sun and Punchbowl, Holborn, and of the
Cock at Sutton. He died on 7 Oct. 1845 at
No. 4 Lower Grosvenor Street West, London,

in his seventy-seventh year, and was buriled in Brompton Cemetery, where a colossal monument was erected by subscription to his memory. Byron, who was one of his pupils, had a great regard for him, and often walked and drove with him in public. It is related that, while the poet was at Cambridge, his tutor remonstrated with him on being seen in company so much beneath his rank, and that he replied that "Jackson's manners were infinitely superior to those of the fellows of the college whom I meet at 'the high table'" (J. W. Clark, Cambridge, 1890, p. 140). He twice alludes to his 'old friend and corporeal pastor and master' in his notes to his poems (Byron, *Poetical Works*, 1885-6, ii. 144, vi. 427), as well as in his 'Hints from Horace' (ib. i. 503):

> And men unpractised in exchanging knocks
> Must go to Jackson ere they dare to box.

Moore, who accompanied Jackson to a prize-fight in December 1818, notes in his diary that Jackson's house was 'a very neat establishment for a boxer', and that the respect paid to him everywhere was 'highly comical' (*Memoirs*, ii. 233). A portrait of Jackson, from an original painting then in the possession of Sir Henry Smythe, bart., will be found in the first volume of Miles's 'Pugilistica' (opp. p. 89). There are two mezzotint engravings by C. Turner.

II.

In Boucicault's *Janet Pride* (revival by Charles Warner at the Adelphi Theatre, London in the early eighties) was sung the following (here given from memory):

The Convict's Song.

The Farewell.

Farewell to old England the beautiful!
Farewell to my old pals as well!
Farewell to the famous Old Ba-i-ly
                              (*Whistle*).
Where I used for to cut sich a swell.
                    Ri-chooral, ri-chooral, Oh!!!

The [Werdhick ?]

These seving long years I've been serving,
    And seving I've got for to stay,
All for bashin' a bloke down our a-alley,
                              (*Whistle*).
    And a' takin' his huxters away!

The Complaint.

There's the Captain, wot is our Commanduer,
    There's the Bosun and all the ship's crew,
There's the married as well as the single 'uns,
                              (*Whistle*).
    Knows wot we pore convicks goes through.

The [Suffering ?]

It ain't' cos they don't give us grub enough,
    It ain't' cos they don't give us clo'es:
It's a-cos all we light-fingred gentery
                              (*Whistle*).
    Goes about with a log on our toes.

The Prayer.

Oh, had I the wings of a turtle-dove,
    Across the broad ocean I'd fly,
Right into the arms of my Polley love
                              (*Whistle*).
    And on her soft bosum I'd lie!

THE MORRELL.

Now, all you young wi-counts and duchesses,
Take warning by wot I've to say,
And mind all your own wot you touches is,
(*Whistle*).
Or you'll jine us in Botinny Bay !
Oh ! ! !

Ri-chooral, ri-chooral, ri-addiday,

Ri-chooral, ri-chooral, iday.